MW01254586

A VERSE

FROM BABYLON

BOOKS BY JEANNELLE M. FERREIRA

DRAMATIS PERSONAE

A VERSE

FROM BABYLON

JEANNELLE M. FERREIRA

PRIME BOOKS

Prime Books
www.prime-books.com

Thanks to Sonya Taaffe for the challenge that completed this book. To my Nicole, for love and support of my artistic temperament. And to all the people along the years who read drafts, commented on character and plot, and helped me become a novelist, including Catherine Durot, Emily Clare Friedman, Kim Godsoe, Lawrence Szenes-Strauss and Terri Machtiger Strauss, Sarah, Sophie, the patrons of Milliways Bar, the patient staff of the United States Holocaust Memorial Museum, and my mother.

Mir leben ibik, oyf di ganze velt.

PROLOGUE

This photograph was never taken. That's the reason it never blurred, though no one in it is still. No one wears the clothes you keep for shul, or the smiles that only come to the face in studios. It's a crowded picture, in good bright color, or maybe someone has taken care to tint it all by hand. Such things were still done, in those days.

This is Vilna in the nineteen-thirties. If Warsaw is the heart of Judaism, Vilna is the muscled right arm, the refined hand, the lively fingers. This is a garden party in Vilna's wealthiest street, and the laughing people, maybe a little drunk, are calling to one another in English, in German, in French. Their accents are good. Their clothes are stylish and clean. They are not beautiful, these people, they look like anyone else anywhere in the world. They do not look like Jews: not at all like the pictures you see in the best evening papers, with the hooked noses, the dark greasy hair and the careful diagrams of how a Jew is supposed to look.

Everyone is young. Everyone has had a haphazard sandwich and a glass of icy dark beer. The children had punch, from a Sevres bowl; the children are there, running barefoot, a game of tag in and out of pine trees. The adults talk. Some are clever, some witty, some wise. They talk and argue, argue and laugh, and sing.

The girl who started the singing was famous, before her marriage brought her here. Now she finds an old song of summer, in a silver soprano said to be not quite of this world, and nostalgic everyone around her joins in. This is her husband, quiet, impassive. That's her baby, swaddled in the basket on the grass.

The young woman with the cherry-stained mouth, there, in the trousers, has written years of love poems, in golden-brown ink; and the one in the poems, she's here, combing dried cherry blossoms from her lover's dark hair. Later this year they're going to Berlin, a long-planned, long-promised trip, with sleeper trains and statues and museums. They'll go together.

With her legs in the river, here, is the fishmonger's daughter, invited up from the town in her very-best pale blue linen; maybe the hem has been twice let down, because this dress was cut for the dark girl beneath the cherry tree, before she drew everyone's eyes by wearing just trousers. The girl who wears it now has knitting beside her, in a calico bag, but her head is turned and she's listening to a boy with a gift for the fiddle. He wears the black cap and narrow black coat of the select yeshiva, but he plays for their dancing, faster, wilder, faster.

Those are his twin's feet, the dark spots in that birch tree; even the feet are shy. The twin has eyeglasses and, recently, an Adam's apple; he has a hungry look and the women in town press on him spice-dark slabs of honey cake. His poems are all written in exercise books beside scraps of Mishnah, and no one has gotten close enough yet to say just what color his eyes are.

Indolent, pensive, merry or longing, they've waited here, at this bend in the river Vilye, in this place and day and picture that never was. They wait for their real lives to start.

None will survive.

AND IN FIRE I SPEND MY DAYS

> "And I do want, God, truly,
> To tell you all my troubles
> But inside me a fire burns,
> And in fire I spend my days.
> In corners and in cellars
> The murderous voice is crying;
> I flee higher, over rooftops,
> And I cry *Where are You, where?*"
> —Abraham Sutzkeyver

In the birch-sheltered lane near the Vilye's bank, a woman stood, reading. She was dressed in black, five years out of the style; her hair was a bright-glinting red, curled at its heavy ends around her chin. She carried about six other books and a large clasp folio against her chest, and it was while noticing all of this that Raissa collided with one of the birch trees, gone unnoticed.

"Ow!" She jumped clear of the bicycle, caught her ankle against the chains and landed in the leaf-moldy gutter, smashing midway into something soft that shrieked. There was an explosion of paper and dead leaves, the dull clatter of books

11

falling into the unpaved road. Raissa half-sat among strewn pens, ink-bottles and a writing tablet now smeared with a bar of chocolate, wincing for skinned places undiscovered yet.

"Watch your bloody velo!"

"Oh, my God, are you all right?" Raissa spat a mouthful of leaves.

Papery gold birch leaves stuck in the stranger's red hair, and one sleeve twisted so that Raissa knew it would be torn, but she got to her feet before Raissa could. "I'm fine. Can you stand up?"

Raissa stared at her. "You speak Yiddish!"

"Mostly."

"I'm sorry, I'm really sorry. No one is ever up here. I didn't think you were real," Raissa finished, slapping at her ankle and trying to shake the hair ribbon from her eyes.

"I've had my own doubts." The woman shook her head, knelt, gathered the books and papers in reach and brushed the worst of the dirt off them.

"That one's mine," ventured Raissa, "I—unless you were reading *Tik-Tok of Oz.*"

Her eyes were a strange deep blue, and even her eyebrows were red. She handed the book to Raissa, in exchange for a sheaf of papers Raissa's elbow had pinned. The folio was mostly sticking out of a muddy crater in the road; Raissa fished it up and wiped the draggled corner clean on her shirt.

"What's your name?" she asked, handing it over. "I'm Raissa, Raissa Gellerman, Sylvie if you want, but I always thought that was kind of affected."

"Violeta."

"What?"

"Name's Violeta."

"That's not a Jewish . . . I mean, aren't you Jewish?"

"Yes, actually. From Kiev."

Raissa stood in her mud-slathered trousers and torn vest, and looked idiotic. "You've just come here, then? Have you seen the river yet? It's gorgeous, just here. The river Vilye."

"No," Violeta replied, so vague that Raissa peered to see what held her attention. " 'And she saw the sea, which she could not understand, and saw instead the lifetime of her own tears'—you wrote this?"

"Oh, God, I'm not very good."

Violeta smiled merely, and did not hand the paper back. "I'd like to finish this."

"Writing it?"

"Reading."

"Um. I. All right."

"When you finish anything else, I'd like to see it."

Raissa stood for a moment after Violeta had gone, under the thin green-gold shelter of the leaves. By her foot there was a torn and crumpled page, better paper than she had ever bought for herself; she picked it up, smoothed it but did not call back to its owner.

[1937]

Eight people waited, not even a minyan.

The library of the Gellerman house, with its vast creaking shelves and vast costly windows, had survived two wars, the Bolsheviks, and three generations of children. Now it seemed to shake, though there was no artillery near, and gold-leaf titles sparked from the shelves like frightened eyes. The velvet curtains were all drawn shut, though outside it might yet have been day.

The ancient oak doors were ajar. What they awaited had force enough to shiver the locks.

Someone had thought to build a fire, because the sky had come down over the city, pallid with unfallen snow. Unheeded, it was dying, into a cave of embers and half-consumed coals. The room was warm enough without it; the room was stifling. No one moved to open the tiny winter-windows hidden in the great leaded panes.

"How long do you think?" Fayge asked, and she turned to Beniek, but it was Mikah Glik who answered. His slender hands rested on the neck of his violin case, untrembling.

"They'll empty the Quarter first."

"But the Ghetto takes up the whole Quarter. I've seen the wires!"

"Doesn't matter. Just to shuffle people up. How many blocks of apartments down there? How many families, block for block?"

"Twenty thousand, maybe." Hirsh lifted his head from the book he devoured.

"Here by evening," Mikah calculated, and turned his brother's page.

"We should go now, before they get here, what's the use in waiting!" Sheyndl, the fish-seller's daughter, eleven in her family and no one had any idea where they were. Her eyes were red-rimmed and her braid was coming loose in tangled hanks. Raissa took her hand, for a second, as long as she could bear letting go of Violeta's.

"I will not go, not until I have no other choice." Beniek sat turned from the firelight, his hair molten gold and his profile a king's. Raissa flinched, unable to look at her eldest brother for long. *Marek, Loniek, Lysiek, Father, Mother, Beryl, Ania: what did we do to you, that you left us here?* Anger made her name the dead with the absent. She curled her fingernails into her palms and would not cry.

She seized a book from the sideboard nearest, and flung it into the fire.

Everyone jumped, and Fayge stifled a scream, and the binding gave a satisfying roar as the flames turned to green.

"Father's in America. He won't feel it."

"Sheyna," Violeta soothed.

"No." Raissa threw off any touch. She stood too quickly, and a thousand thousand knives struck into the curve of her spine. Pain would have knocked her from her feet, but there was more relief in anger than in falling. "You tell them, Beni; tell them all about Father, and don't leave out Lysander, either, or Mother."

"Sha," he stopped her, and no one who heard it could tell whether it was comfort or command. The baby stirred, in Fayge's lap, and the room was still.

"Oh, but you should, it's the best joke in the world."

"Raissa, you'll make yourself sick."

"Tell your wife, at least, Beni. One visa for the eldest son, the darling, golden, good; but none, somehow, for his wife or for his child." She paused. "That must have been Lysander's idea, don't you think? He never did like foreigners."

"No," Beniek replied. He was standing, the whole room filled with his shadow, and under it Raissa shrank. "And so here we are."

She waited for him to strike her.

"You should have gone, with the girls," Beniek muttered, "you, the youngest, he should have thought of you. But here we are." His pale agate eyes were softer, suddenly, bright at the corners as Raissa had never seen; it took her several breaths to realize he was crying. He pulled her against his shirt front, hard, and kissed the top of her head. Raissa hugged him fiercely back.

"Sit down," he told her, "before you fall." His face was red to the hairline, though Raissa could not tell, with her glasses so misted, whether he was angry or afraid or acutely embarrassed. No one said anything, though Violeta's face was hidden in the fall of her hair, and Fayge concentrated on the phoenix-tail whorls of the carpet.

An hour had passed, or three hours, and no one thought of food. Dusk crept into the library's corners; Hirsh brought his book to the fireside, and Mikah came with him. Sheyndl stared ahead, Beniek toyed with his sleeping daughter's hair, and against Raissa's neck Violeta whispered something like psalms. The clock ticked, and even struck, for a while. Raissa got up, wordless, and unlocked the case and made the pendulum still. No one stopped her; no one moved. She dropped the clock key into a crack in the floor.

From the pocket of his long black coat Hirsh took another book, smaller, the black binding beaten and worn down to gray. The pages ruffled and splayed, with the softest possible noise, and Sheyndl shrieked.

"No, no, it makes me feel already dead—"

"Sunset," Hirsh cut her off, mildly. "Sunset, whether they're coming or not. If it upsets you, we'll pray in our heads."

"Please." Violeta startled all of them. "Not in your heads. I mean, out loud. If you would."

"Vi," Raissa squeezed her hand. "I'm scared."

"So am I, sheyna, so am I."

It was full dark, purplish winter dark with piercing winter stars, when the fall of boots made Beniek turn his head. There were soldiers on the white gravel drive, maybe twenty, maybe fifty; he steepled his fingers under his chin, the dull gold of his wedding band shot a sudden gleam, and Raissa could hear them, hollow, heavy, on the granite steps before the door.

Someone knocked, and behind her eyelids Raissa could see perfectly a black leather glove, gripping the bar in the great bronze lion's mouth.

What came next could not be called a knock, but Beniek didn't move.

"Beni, please, for God's sake, just open the door . . . " It was Fayge, begging, one delicate hand on his sleeve; no one else could find their voices, yet.

Five men abreast, easily, pounding and beating and on the second floor, with the soaring stair and carpet-muffled passages between them, Raissa knew the door screamed protest, and started to bend.

"Beniek," she said, around the numb encumbrance of her fear. "Beniek, open the door."

*

Naked they came into the ghetto.

Raissa stripped fast, hairpins and linen and all, and lay down with her cheek to the earth and a bored expression, one arm crooked over her discarded clothes. She set her teeth together when the hands came down on her, and took a few kicks for having no gold, no diamonds, no screams. Next to her Violeta stared at the sky, corpse-still with snow settling into her hair.

"Gets almost routine, doesn't it?"

"You hurt, Vi?"

"No. Cold maybe."

"Aw, shit, Beni's wife, the wedding ring, shit!" Raissa, almost fast enough, shoved her fingers in her ears.

When the order came for them to stand, she did; not too quickly, and with careful disregard for her own nakedness and everyone else's. Fayge's left hand streamed blood, and Hirsh's mouth, and God above knew what they'd done to Mikah's face, kicked his eyeglasses in, maybe, but they were alive.

"State your name, age and profession."

The word for this officer, Raissa thought, *is shiny: shiny hair, shiny coat, shiny bloody chin from so many wursts . . .*

Fayge was not crying. Her voice was steady and cold, and

17

she answered before Raissa could. "Silverberg Gellerman, Fayge, nineteen, singer."

"Gellerman, Raissa Sylvie, twenty-one, writer."

"Markiewics, Ariel, twenty-five, linguist."

"Hirsh Kadosh Glik, twenty-three, writer."

"Mikah Ionas Glik, twenty-three, composer."

"Gellerman, Benyamin, thirty-five, theatrical director."

"Fucking Christ, are all of you lot fucking artists? Seven fucking adult Jews without a trade!"

"Let 'em get dressed," someone said from behind Raissa's left ear. "Let them through. There's some God-cursed rumor we're supposed to start the Jews a theatre; these might as well be it. Rich, artsy Jews! Know any Shakespeare, you fucking artists?"

"Nah, Herr Oberscharführer, with the goddamn Jews it's all Brecht . . . "

"This is bad," Violeta hissed.

"We're not dead." Raissa pulled her shirt on as she ran, barefoot and stumbling, through the ghetto gate. "It's not bad yet."

[August 1941]

They entered the theatre silently, first Beniek with the keys, then Raissa, Violeta, Hirsh and Mikah, Sheyndl with the bundle of rotting costumes, Leyb and Chaya and Fayge. It was a cavern, a tomb, a shadowed tattered shipwreck; the dark was heavy and the air cold, as ice is cold in dreams.

"Cheerful," Mikah pronounced.

"Please, some light!"

It was still summer outside, and Raissa stifled a shiver. "It's not dark, Chaya'le. The windows are high, up there, look."

"That wasn't me, that was Leyb!"

"Leyb's voice should break then."

"He should live so long." It was Hirsh, because Mikah

18

clipped him on the shoulder and almost at once, the brothers were scuffling.

"Door's stuck," Beniek cursed into the dark. "It wouldn't be so bad, some light."

"Is it still our theatre, do you suppose, if we never get past the lobby?"

Sheyndl plumped the bundle of silk and brocade onto the marble floor, and sat down on it, a long disgusted sigh in place of idea or opinion.

"Fucking hell." Raissa said it for the small pleasure of pinkening Fayge's ears, though she could not see anyone's ears for dusk and dust. "Give me a hand up, Hirshke." She stood under one of the boarded-dark windows and waited for Hirsh to follow.

"Asthma," he said, and "sorry."

"You just don't want my feet on your shoulders."

He shot back, "Damn right!"

"Mikah—"

"I'm coming, I'm coming. One twin's as good as another, I guess." His shadow stooped near her, and then his white hand differentiated itself from his black woolen coat. He was sweating in it, even now, but neither brother had ever been seen without one. Raissa, in her stockings, scrambled from his palm to his shoulder and from there, after a second's struggle, she managed to crouch on the window's deep sill.

"It smells like hell in here, Rai."

"It's not too much better from up here."

"It won't smell like roses inside, either," said Hirsh. "They did the first round from here, didn't they? Seven thousand people, for three days?"

"*Pas devant les enfants.*" It was Violeta, icily, and Hirsh shut up.

"We're not children!"

"You are."

Raissa threw the first board down into the gloom, into sudden silence. A muted sunlight shot into the lobby, enough for her to see by, enough to make her eyes water. From here she could see over the barbed wire, out to the river, and up to the pine-thick hills . . .

There were no more trees on the Ninth Fort Hill.

She tore away another board, blinked hard into the light, and reached into her breast pocket for her glasses.

Some small noise came past her teeth, and she prayed it lost in the cave of the ceiling. Where the trees had been, there were long black gashes in the earth; and the pines were piled, on fire, burning with a low and terrible smoke.

"All right up there? Raissa?"

With a wrench the last board came free, unbalancing her with it; she swayed out into the open air, and never knew how she righted. She should come down. The others waited.

The hill burned.

"Sheyna, are you hurt?"

"I . . . " Raissa turned, and what she had meant to say was gone. Chaya was holding Leyb's hand, and they had twenty years if you added them both together, and God knew where their parents were. God, and Raissa, and the men in the fort on the hill. She jumped down, caught, safe between Mikah and Beniek. She said not a word.

*

"I don't remember it ever being this hot. Ever." Raissa had wedged herself into the window, to catch any stale sign of a river breeze; feeling grimy and vulnerable she dropped back down into the apartment.

"It confirms what I've long suspected, you know." Violeta paused, resting her pen on her front teeth, but Raissa was too languid to take the bait. "This is just some little suburb of hell, and one day soon we'll just fall straight in."

"Saves them the trouble of burning us alive."

"Ah, sheyna, don't talk like that."

"Sorry," Raissa scuffed along a crack in the floor, to keep from Violeta's eyes, but it was quicker to look up, anyway, and face them. "You're pale, Violeta."

Violeta sat far from the sunlight; still there was sweat in the hollow of her throat, and her cropped red hair dampened blood-colored at the ends. "I was born pale. And if not that, sheyna, then it's only the heat." She closed her eyes for a moment, and held out a hand. "Come, sit, it's not so bad over here."

"I think it's worse." Away from the one narrow window the air hung limp and real as any curtain. Raissa fidgeted, rolled up her trouser legs, would have rolled her sleeves if she had any. "I can't just sit, beloved, I can't. Let me go for water, or something."

"If a breeze comes, I'll save half for you. And then you've got to listen to this one, I think it might even be some good."

"Your poems are always good. Like going to the cinema and getting a Mickey Mouse besides."

"Thanks," Violeta called, though her voice parched halfway and cracked.

*

"Ice? Sheyna, where in hell did you get ice?"

"Where does anyone get anything?" Raissa shrugged. She hung up her shirt, wrung through with sweat, and stood in the windowsill bare to the waist, with a piece of ice pressed to her neck.

Violeta dipped a cautious hand into their water bucket. "More than half full of ice, in the middle of Poland in the middle of a war?"

"In the middle of a ghetto." Raissa jumped down.

"It was your Pushkin, wasn't it, you sold the Pushkin—"

"Violeta, shhh." Their tiny room shimmered with heat, and silver beads were sliding from the bucket, running to pool along the desk's edge. But Violeta drew her hands back from the ice.

"Your books," Violeta started.

"Your books, too. Shut up." She kissed Violeta, who always kissed first. It was too hot to shout, to hold on to each other, to cry. There was an airless scuffling moment, and then Raissa got some small grip on the bucket's edge.

Drenched, one of them screamed and one of them squawked. Violeta fell, laughing, and ice in pieces skittered over the floor. Raissa shivered a little, shook the cold water from her ears and pounced on the shard of ice nearest her hand.

"You don't dare, you don't—ah—" Violeta put up her arms, but Raissa was quicker; with the ice, and with the kiss. A cool path for her mouth to trace, down Violeta's throat, her famine-sharp collarbones, and then the ice melted into the rough wet edge of Violeta's shirt. Raissa fumbled, and tore at it, and only realized when Violeta's hand closed on hers that she was working with her eyes shut.

Violeta's voice, gentle, uneven. "No one's going to catch you looking."

If Raissa blushed, that wasn't so strange, in all this heat. Violeta was there, shell-pale, familiar, and if she laughed, it was softly, and ended in " . . . Please."

She bent her head to Violeta's breast and tasted sweat like river water, half sweet, half salt. Her weight was all on one wrist and under her palm, ice melted, forgotten; her own hair came down around them both, shadowing everything, cerise and white. Violeta moaned, and there were words in it, but Raissa lost them. She was learning again how lips and nipple fit, and she could not have moved, not even to breathe, Violeta's hands were so deep in her hair.

"Beloved," Violeta gasped. Sliding, shifting between the floor and the wall, so that her skin was a blurred pale red to Raissa's eyes, she finished her sentence in Hebrew or Russian or French. Raissa stirred, and the band of Violeta's skirt was against her teeth, and in her head she stopped translating.

It took her a moment's breathing, silent, sweat-blind. There were four buttons to the waist, and nothing underneath.

"Oh. God." Or something like that. Something. She knew when Violeta's knee brushed over her shoulder, still half tangled, for a second, in the skirt. Caught in heat and scent she faltered, because it had been so long, she thought, *because death is waiting at the door, for both of us, and her red hair, God, that red hair, she's beautiful and it still won't save her and I can't save her and I can't . . . .*

"Rais'le?"

She kissed the curve of Violeta's thigh, tasting her own tears and then only Violeta. Faintly sweet, and familiar, hot and drenching against her cheek and she knew the way, with her eyes closed, from here. Quick with her tongue as her lover quickened, she sought; she moved with the tide pull of Violeta's hips, slicked, suckling, needing to taste but not to breathe. She answered, when Violeta cried out, though what she whispered came silent in the press of skin on skin.

The world was hot and still. Under her cheek, Violeta's pulse thrummed. Somewhere, angry mare's heads lowered across the sky and somewhere, there might be rain; Violeta's fingers twisted in Raissa's damp hair, and they were alive.

[September 1941]

"Where's Mikah?"

"No idea," said Hirsh, and in his eyes Raissa caught a tiny spark of worry. "He was gone before I woke up. I thought to find him here with you."

"Where's Fayge and Beniek, for that matter?" Sheyndl asked. "Not that I mind the crowd in here being a bissele thinner."

"Beni's down the Judenrat, something about our rations. I've decided, better I don't know so well where's his wife."

"Speak with a fragment of your education, please, sheyna, you'll make me look bad." Violeta grinned and pulled Raissa against her.

"Why should it reflect on you, what comes out of her big mouth?"

"Oh, spill your ink, Hirshke."

"No, I mean it. I haven't seen Vi smile for months, so what's the joke?"

"She taught me all the boring subjects at the Gymnasium."

"It's true, she taught maths for a year . . . and hard enough marks she gave me. I wasn't good enough to get in her grammar class, though." Sheyndl looked thoughtful, with a slight narrowing of her good-natured green eyes. "Rais'le, I never saw you together," she argued at last. "And I was with you 'most all the time."

"Not when you were knocking teeth with Itzhak Horowicz."

"You wouldn't have seen us together," Violeta said. "Forgive me your algebra marks, all right?"

"I don't forgive you for mine," Raissa laughed.

Hirsh looked reproachful, behind his glasses. "To think how I suffered for you, Rais'le, and you never told me: you wouldn't go with me because you were too busy gawping at Teacher."

Raissa said, simply, "Hirshke, you didn't have red hair."

"Tits either."

"It went the other way, Hirsh, be fair; I thought she was beautiful." Violeta grinned. "Read too much Novalis, but beautiful."

"Oy, Violeta." Raissa ducked into the curve of her lover's arm.

"No kissing, in God's name. I'm hungry, I'm tired, my knees are stuck sitting, I don't need abominations right in front of me."

They did not kiss, but only because Raissa lifted her head at the last second, to listen.

"What's that . . . "

"Don't go home!" The fire door slammed and Fayge was on their side of it. She gestured, breathless, her hands twisting uselessly in the air; she tried, in Yiddish, to say something and stopped.

"Speak German." Violeta stood up. "Breathe, Fayge, and tell us."

"You can't leave. They've closed off Rodnitzki all the way to the gate, and they're taking every third person, doctors, Jewish Police, they don't care. Straight on the trucks."

"How did you get here, then?"

Fayge shrugged.

"On the trolley, of course," Raissa said dryly. "Where's your armband, Aryaner?"

"Shut up, sheyna."

Every head in the room turned. Violeta had crossed the room, and stood closer to Fayge than anyone else.

"I have no right to ask this, of anybody," she said, low. "But if you would go out there again and see . . . what the fuss is about . . . I would be grateful."

Fayge set down her rucksack and nodded. "Grateful, never mind that. I don't much care for the air in here, anyway." She twitched her skirt neat, and tilted her gray felt hat, and gave the room a dazzling smile and the rucksack a little kick. "Lunch. And don't eat all the herring. I need it to pay my fine at the library."

"That girl's wrong in the head." Hirsh was blushing from her smile. "Still, she brought lunch."

Raissa stared at the lump of potato bread and the finger-slim piece of smoked herring, without taking a bite, until Violeta pushed it towards her. "Don't be such a jealous little fool. Besides, the herring's delicious."

"You eat it."

"Stop this," Violeta hissed. "You had no reason to say such things to her. But food is food, so forget it, and eat."

"Hirsh isn't so hungry either, maybe," Sheyndl said around a mouthful of fish.

"I just thought . . . for Mikah . . . "

"Eat it." Violeta shook her head. "Eat, and don't think, for God's sake. I'm tired of watching your elbows poke holes in that coat."

Some wrong note in her words made Raissa look up; but Violeta's dark-flecked eyes were empty and cool, and just as quickly she was counting the smoke-burnished scales of the herring.

"I tell you what, Hirsh, Mikah's got some girl pregnant, and he's off the other side of the ghetto leading a what-you-call-it, a double life."

"Who's he going to get pregnant? Nobody's bled in months."

Hirsh, his ears the color of wild strawberries, mumbled something and got up from the worktable.

"You know exactly where Mikah's gone," Raissa whispered, fierce accusation. "You know what's going on, or you guess. And you won't tell me!"

"Be still, sheyna."

"Oh, don't give me that!"

"Be still," Violeta repeated, "because, forgive me, Raissa, I would rather not see you hung."

"If you're going to fight, I'll be . . . I don't know, somewhere else," said Sheyndl. "My nerves are bad enough, before people start fighting. So—so I'm going over stage left somewhere, and don't fight too damn loud." Gathering up the peasant costume she was altering, she sidled away from them, though she could not go farther for light's sake than the edge of the stage.

"Are we going to fight?"

"What for, sheyna, because I was kind to that poor girl?"

Raissa looked down at her hands. The plain silvery-dull iron band Mikah had made for her three years ago, in secret, was still there; on her thumb, now, because she feared it would slip and be lost. After all the screaming with Lysiek, with Father; after Berlin, and after all this time . . .

Violeta had kept hers, too, even when they broke all the fingers of her left hand. Raissa had never asked her how.

"I've never given you cause to mistrust me, and I will not. Ever."

The north fire door opened again before Raissa could speak. There was a too-long space of silence, and no shadow crossed the rectangle of dim dirty light from the street. She burst out, unthinking, "Mikah?"

Fayge closed it, softly this time.

"Tonight will be bad," she said. "Violeta, they got away."

*

"Twenty men aren't worth an Aktion," protested Raissa.

"Twenty men with guns are." Violeta was on her knees among the wardrobe trunks, sifting aside kings, caliphs,

27

Hasid's coats. "Almighty God, is there not a dress in here for her to wear?"

"Those are the men's costumes."

Violeta scowled.

"How is she so sure there'll be one, anyway?"

"She asked someone who knew." Violeta would not come near catching Raissa's gaze.

"I just don't think it likely, I mean, some poor bastards got over the wire, let's spend the whole night shooting Jews, like last October?"

"Sheyna, twenty strong, healthy, armed, pissed-off Jewish men are out there somewhere in the woods, and if they made it, then there are more. Try to understand why the Germans are afraid."

"You helped them." Raissa sank onto a trunk, heedless whether it was open or closed. "That's why the Judenrat wanted you to teach a Russian class. They've gone to the border, haven't they, to the Russians?"

"Before God I hope so."

"You could hope it there before too long, if Fayge's right . . . "

"She's right."

"Violeta, oh, God, they'll find you. If they know who these men are, they'll go to the Judenrat and find your name."

"What name will they find, sheyna?" Violeta smiled, with enough nerve and flint and fear to make Raissa sick. "Come on. A dress. Before Beniek sees her, and throws a clot."

"Wha—why should Beniek care if Fayge tore her dress?"

"Use your brain, Rais'le!"

"Oh." Raissa thought back to Fayge standing, a little dazed, a little triumphant, in the shadows by the fire door: torn skirt and laddered stockings and blood lining her pretty lips. "She's not, Vi, she's not fucking one of them?"

"Of course she is. I would too, if I could profit by it."

"Beniek would kill her if he found out . . . "

"Beniek would starve to death if she didn't." Violeta held a dress up for scrutiny. It was too long for any of them, but whole and mostly clean. "Bring this to her. Here."

"Vi, if it is going to be an Aktion, what are we going to do?"

"I'm trying to figure that out." Violeta put her arms over Raissa's shoulders and kissed her, quickly. "I'll figure something out."

*

"I don't see what's to figure out." Fayge was washing her face, as best as it could be done with a handkerchief and the saucepot someone had placed to catch a ceiling leak. "Forgive me, don't inhale that, it's Luminal."

Violeta put the top back on the flask.

"Drink's in the silver one. Vile, and I cannot pronounce it, but it works."

"May—"

"Help yourself."

When the choking subsided and the fire had left her lungs, Violeta continued. "Raissa and I, our papers won't stand up in an Aktion. We're criminals."

"We're all criminals." Fayge's smile twisted. "You've just got the special stamp in your passport. What do the numbers mean, anyway?"

"They mean . . . " Violeta took back her papers, and ran a finger across the thick-inked numbers that cut through the photograph. "That under oath we would not deny each other."

Fayge, now half-sitting on the table, looked up from the silk stocking she was trying to save. "What? That's it? I thought, to hear Beniek talk, you went to Berlin and did a murder or something."

"We were in Berlin, yes. The charge, as I remember it, was conspiracy to commit politically subversive acts."

"And that was it, you could have said, nah, I'm the least subversive person I know, and they would have let you go home? By God, they make them real idiots in the East. Or braver," Fayge said after a moment, considering. "You shouldn't worry, you know, about tonight."

"I don't worry for myself."

"You shouldn't for Raissa, either. It does no good. If they want to kill her, she'll die, same as my daughter or me or anybody else."

"I beg your pardon," Violeta said. "No."

Sitting on the tabletop, swinging her legs, Fayge could just make her pale blue eyes even with Violeta's. She waited, closed-mouthed, very eloquently.

"I saw her broken, once. They snapped her spine like kindling. I thought she had died, and I died with her. Not again, not while I'm alive, is there anything in those words you don't understand?"

"Glass-clear," said Fayge. "Crystal." She slid off the table. Without her heels, she reached the top button of Violeta's shirt. "You really love each other, don't you?"

Violeta breathed the strange mingled scents of lavender water and castoff clothes, bewildered; and then Fayge had stepped back.

"Sometimes, I think, I love my husband." Fayge shrugged. "Stay here and you'll be all right. They won't search the theatre."

"But why—"

"Because I've told them it's empty. They'll listen to me, because I talk like them and I look like them and I let them fuck me and what do you care, anyway? It's my neck."

Violeta stared at her. Fayge was curling a strand of her honey-colored hair around one finger, and standing on the outside of her shoes, looking sixteen-years-old with eyes of sixty. She projected nothing but complete ease, and Violeta wanted to stop herself from speaking then, because she knew she'd say nothing that would help or change or not already be icicle-clear in Fayge's own head.

"Faygelein," she said, and watched the girl tense under the endearment quick as if it had been a lash. "You are in this way past your neck."

[October 1941]

The rehearsal had stretched past all the daylight, and in the theatre it was too cold for the s to move, and the singers were silent where cold pierced their jaws. It was grim-quiet except for the shuffle and scuffle of papers, down in the orchestra pit, and Violeta's small clear soprano as she fit words to the week's tunes.

"Quiet! Please, a little quiet!"

"Heat, please, a little heat!"

Everyone on the stage turned to squint down at the writers. Violeta lobbed a bottle of frozen ink. Hirsh clapped his gloved bony hands together, and Raissa coughed hard into her handkerchief.

"It's colder than the far side of hell down here, Beni!"

"Come up here then."

"And be tap-danced to death. No, thank you. You might see about getting us some coal," Raissa complained.

"Or just some moldy straw with piss on it, at least we could burn that."

"Burn your mistakes," Beniek shouted down to them, and Violeta smiled, against the end of her pen, but Hirsh looked blackly from behind his glasses.

"Go home, go on, get out of it," Raissa swatted across the table. "Leave us in peace."

"But if you can find some of that moldy straw, come back with it."

Hirsh shrugged farther into his coat, but did not leave the table. He brought two bottles of ink from against his chest, where they had been warming. Violeta and Raissa took one between them, since there was nothing to do but keep on writing.

"What do you want to do after the war?" Raissa tucked her work neatly as possible under the river stones that strewed the table. Without weights a strong gust through the building would scatter paper, and she never remembered to number her pages.

"I want to go into the cake shop on Strashunaya and eat everything I see."

"No, Hirshke, I don't mean like that." She slid from the bench, out of sight under the table, and rummaged for a minute before reappearing. "Here, since you had to talk about food."

There were three pieces of army biscuit, specked slightly with lint, wrapped in newspaper. Hirsh handed them round, and kept the newsprint.

"It's old," he said after a minute's chewing.

"The hardtack or the news?" Raissa shrugged. "So tell us, after the war . . . ?"

"I would like to see my brother," Hirsh said, blinking and blinking. "And then I would go as a soldier, in Palestine."

"Hirshke, you're blind as half a bat. You couldn't shoot."

"I can shoot!"

The table jumped, as Violeta trod on his foot. "What about you, sheyna?"

Raissa sucked at the edge of her biscuit. "Writer," she said, "Auberge of our own. Lyons."

"I want to translate Marlowe into Yiddish," Violeta said, softly but without prompting. "Shakespeare too, let's be fair."

"Shakespeare too," Hirsh echoed, partly a laugh. "Golden lads and girls all must, as chimney-sweepers, come to dust . . . "

"It's a good tune," said Violeta.

"He made it up himself, just this second." Raissa grinned. "Ask him."

"It's from 'Cymbeline'," he protested.

"I meant the tune, and you know I meant the tune. You're wasted as a poet, Hirshke, you might as well go up to the piano and admit it."

"Yes, go, and strangle the pianist while you're up there. Or at least tell him to tune." Violeta frowned. "See if they've got their words right yet, for the patter song."

"They can hardly help it if they don't. The altos both got shot."

"That's got nothing to do with their words," Hirsh muttered, as he climbed up from the pit.

When he had gone Violeta dropped out of sight, and Raissa followed. In among the table legs and rucksacks it was warmer, for a moment, and Violeta curled up with her head on Raissa's breast.

"I'm tired," she whispered.

"Then sleep." Raissa took Violeta's hands and drew them under her shirt, shrugging her jacket over them both. "I'm here. You can sleep."

"Rais'le."

"Mm?"

"What do you want, for after the war? After all this. Really."

"I don't know. I can't see that far."

"I can, sometimes." Violeta sighed. "Only sometimes."

"What's there?"

"A university. A library. A place of our own, where we can just, I don't know, just be."

"I've never heard you say that," Raissa thought, without meaning to speak.

"Say what?"

" 'I don't know'."

"I don't," Violeta said.

"I love you."

Violeta pulled her down and kissed her, a hot blur of a kiss. "I don't know, anymore, except I love you. And . . . and I think I'm so tired, beloved, I'm forgetting half my words."

"I got the sense of it all right." Raissa combed the hair back from Violeta's forehead. "Sleep."

The groaning of the great doors woke them, and they sat up, together, when the fire doors on every side clanged shut.

"Fuck." Violeta shoved Raissa's arms into her jacket.

"It can't be," Raissa gulped. "They can't be here. They can't."

"Line up! Form fives!"

"They can, I think."

"Vi, oh God. Vi . . . "

"Your papers are in order. They can't do anything to us that they haven't done already. And maybe they're just here for a nice game of scare the fuck out of the Jews." Violeta jumped onto the stage, and hauled Raissa up after her.

They were noticed. Raissa felt herself swung around, but Violeta had not let go of her hand, and when she fell, she took Violeta's fall in her stomach.

"You are late, Jews!"

"Gellerman," she managed, her teeth chattering. "Raissa Sylvie. We were down there, sir, we were working. We were."

The officer did not look at her papers. He was an officer, she could tell from the lightning bolts on the black; but the rank escaped her, and then speaking escaped her, at all.

"Get up! Stand up!"

Violeta's hand in hers gripped harder, and they were not torn apart.

"Get in line, if you can count to five."

One of them stumbled, and the other held her up.

"Papers out!"

They were in line, like everybody else.

"Ariel Markiewicz, called Stern!"

"Violeta, oh God, oh God, oh God . . . "

"Where is Ariel Markiewicz Stern?"

There was a shot, and somebody fell.

"Violeta!"

There was a shot, and somebody fell.

"For previous convictions under the Reich penal code, Ariel Markiewicz Stern!"

There was a shot, and somebody fell.

"Beloved, let go, beloved, it's all right."

The pistol muzzle came still hot against Raissa's ear.

She screamed, and Violeta let go of her hand.

[December 1941]

I.

Teach me with kisses what my eyes speak . . .

Someone, singing. The phrasing was all right, she thought, half drowsing, before the voice itself made her start up from the firelit pillows, before she remembered. A wireless. On the other side of the bed, he had turned on the wireless. It spared them talking.

She thought of the man who was not with her in the bed. When they met, she was young and needed a sun to orbit; he was golden and tall and kissed her hands through her gloves. A fine dancer, she remembered, when the mood took him for dancing; a poet, a little, though he said he had a sister who was better. He liked to hear her sing more than he liked to hear her talk. When she ran from Vienna, rather than sing wearing the Star, she found him waiting. He had a company, a small one, they were going to try in Paris. The Star was no great matter. He was wearing one himself.

In Paris her life started: no small thing, to be sixteen and dancing with silver powder across her shoulders, to be sixteen and filling the house at the Opera Garnier. Benyamin Gellerman's company got very good notices, and to her his company seemed good. She knew nothing, and he knew less, and he had her with child inside of six months. She was flat on her back in Paris while they broke windows in her home town, burning as the shops and temples burned. She never screamed, not once, lest she shatter her instrument and be nothing.

Her daughter was the sky, the stars and every kind of music, but all the screams stayed in Fayge's throat for months after that. She would not sing, not lullabies, not even when he begged.

East she had come, when he asked it, because he was kind to her and denied her nothing, because he was Miriam's father. East in a train compartment filled with coal grit, and she had ripped the Star from her coat and found it did not matter, because it had left a dark mark in the wool. He gave her his raincoat to wear. She would be the lady of a fine house, in this eastern city she had never heard of, and there were two repertory theatres there, and she would sing.

War came. Men from her own city brought it, and she sang. She did not wear the Star, and armbands could be pulled off in the dark. The men looked at her like a gem.

Her husband did not look at her, the better not to see her starving. He brought her an extra cardigan, pins for her too-long hair, but he could not bring bread. She sang for soldiers—for Miriam, every note on every breath, Miriam, *spur nur dich, spur nur dich allein*—in rooms where her husband could not hear.

She thought of bread, of hot soup and hot featherbeds, of how much blood there is in a man. She thought of her wordless daughter.

She thought of the man beside her, in this bed.

She thought she would lose her mind.

PLATES OF LEAD,
PLATES OF GOLD

. . . And once more we opened the seal
To some kind of secret, eternal cave.
Shielded by shadows, working by flashlight,
We poured the letters—measure by measure,
As our grandfathers once in the Temple
Had poured oil into gilded menorahs.
The lead blazed as the bullets were poured out,
Thoughts—dissolving letter by letter.
A verse of Babylon, a verse of Poland . . .

—A. Sutzkeyver,
'Blayene Platn fun Romms Derkerai'

"Squalid, but . . . "

"No. Just squalid."

"Show some cheer, brother, for God's sake."

Hirsh balanced on the edge of the iron bedstead. On the floor was one torn, dark-stained mattress. There was nothing else in the room, not even the room to turn around when both of them stood abreast. "What do you think happened to them, to the people who lived here?"

"I think they're going to come back after the war and ask us what the hell we're doing living in their closet, because there's no way this is actually a room."

"It's the address on the Judenrat billet," Hirsh shrugged.

"Right. Well, then, I get the bed."

"All right, then I get the mattress!"

"You get your cubic meter of space and the window. The mattress goes with the bed. I'm oldest," Mikah added, after a moment's thought.

"Oy, by ten minutes!"

"Hirshke, I was kidding. Only let me find a place for the violin, and I'll go and see about mattresses. They're all over the ground, out there."

"Don't forget your papers," Hirsh said. His voice was a sliver, a nothing, and he looked down at a knot in the floor. One hand balanced him and his rucksack on his narrow iron perch, and the other hand trembled. Mikah knew better than to talk, or to touch; he put his worn tweed cap on, remembered his papers, and locked the door.

It was still harvest summer, and curfew would not fall for two hours yet. Mikah kept his head down and the neat white blaze of the armband always visible on his sleeve, and no one troubled him where he walked.

The cemetery was within the wire. Greened-over, leaning, cracked and bullet-spangled headstones, the dead crowded up as the living were now; and nowhere among them his sister, or her baby, or their parents. His brother had seen them, sometimes, in dreams, standing expectant in a forest or a field. It sounded enough like a forest-name, Treblinka.

Mikah had tried to dream of them, fearing none of the things Hirsh had feared, and had succeeded not at all. So Hirsh had the visions and tremors and dreams, and Mikah was out in the warm night, in the faint rain, hunting mattresses; and that was all right. Even here against the cemetery gates, there were mattresses like rafts capsized in the mud. Suitcases, too, school satchels and bulging valises, and Mikah was busy enough picking his way through the maze of them to trip over a rain-soaked cardboard carton.

"Books," he said, smiling before he even got onto his feet.

The Gellermans had been billeted on Strashun, because money was money and Beniek knew precisely when to spend it; more uphill than he would have liked, with a disintegrating box squashing at every step against his chest, but the apartment was only on the second floor. Sometime between this war and the last it would have been called an efficiency; it had two windows, a sink and a small patent stove and was about the size of the Gellermans' dining room. The door was open flat against the inner wall, propped by a steamer trunk, and Mikah knocked on the lintel.

"It's open!"

"Ladies," said Mikah, and tipped his cap and dropped the books.

Violeta came to gather them up, in spite of all the protests he meant to make; she was mostly covered in soot, but she found a clean spot on the apron she wore and rubbed her palms skin-colored again before touching the books.

"We hadn't looked for visitors. Forgive us." She was quiet but not grave, and she looked at him, with those eyes black-flecked blue, and seemed pleased. No one in the world was supposed to have eyes a color like that.

"I can't stay long. It's just, I found these, and I know if you leave Raissa without books for very long, she starts to chew things."

"Mm, and you should see what she does to the carpet."

"Books! I can smell them!"

Mikah had not seen Raissa until she shouted; she stood on a chair by the far window, obscured by folds and billows of the curtain she was trying to hang.

"Hey, Vi, come on, let me down from here!"

Violeta stood, with half a grin for him. "Greet your brother for me," she said, already turning. "And take care of yourself, Mikah."

*

"Do you really think it's right, doing this?"

"I don't have to think it's right, I only have to accept it. Don't sing, Raissa."

"I'm not singing, I'm humming."

"Your humming's as bad as your singing." Beniek frowned. "Morality has nothing to do with it. If they want a theatre, and it keeps my wife and Mir'ele alive, then they'll have theatre. They'll have singing and dancing and goddamn juggling, if they tell me that has to be."

Mikah looked up from the canvas he was basting together. It looked more like a sail attacked by a myopic surgeon than a curtain, but for two days now he had persisted. "I think Raissa has a perfectly nice voice, and she can't help if she's tone-deaf."

Hirsh snorted, and went back to lettering a poster. "We have professionals for the singing. All she has to do is come up with some nice, rhymey words."

"Violeta rhymes them for me, actually."

"Gives us something to do in bed at night."

"This is all ludicrous enough without you two nattering back and forth!"

"You natter your fair share, Hirshke." Raissa went to him, and drew his well of red ink out of reach, gently. "Look. I think the idea of live theatre—here—now—is the most painful and sacrilegious and disgusting thing in the world. But it gives us papers, and we stay alive." She studied his poster, for the first time. "Go and burn that, for God's sake, before you get us all killed."

"What had he written?" Mikah asked, when Hirsh had gone. His voice and gaze were mild as ever, but there was a crease between his brows where none had been before.

" 'In A Cemetery Can Be No Theatre.' "

"Never mind." Violeta propped her feet on Hirsh's empty chair. "What was it you just said, sheyna, about papers? Hm."

Half an hour later she sat upright, nudging Mikah with her foot. "Put a tune to that."

"Usually, mademoiselle, I—I do it the other way around."

"Yes, well, try, because they want a show out of us by the nineteenth."

Amiably Mikah shrugged. "What kind of a tune?"

"Find one. See."

" 'Colored papers, pink and yellow; yellow saves your life; I've got my yellow papers, but I haven't got a wife . . . ' Who's going to, I mean, who's the tune for?"

Violeta looked back at him, and so did Raissa, silent, and Mikah spent a long time adjusting his spectacles on his nose.

"Oh. No. I won't do it. Get Hirsh to do it, get someone off the street! I'm not singing. No."

"You have to! Hirsh sounds like a head cold with a head cold!"

"You could do it, Violeta. I've seen you wear a suit, even the tails."

"Are you mad? Beniek would fall in a fit before he let me near his wife, on a stage or no."

"She'd fall in a fit first," Raissa added.

"Um," he said, and went back to the lyrics. "There's Leyb."

"He's ten!"

"A very sturdy ten . . . "

"And a soprano!"

[September 1941]

The house lights were still on, blinding all of them and making a faint hot smell rise from the velvet-covered seats. The theatre was empty, or nearly, but the house didn't matter so much when there were ten black-uniformed Germans treading the stage.

In the center of the stage there was a table, and on the table was bread, cheese, oranges, grapes, a pineapple, a cold-meats tray, vodka, chocolate, caviar and six magnums of champagne. The food was not a mirage, the drink was real; so were the service revolvers half-holstered at the officers' waists.

None of the actors moved. None of the singers bent to those gleaming glasses, or poured from the bottles, to wet their throats. Raissa sidled closer to Violeta, and Fayge ducked behind her husband, and Hirsh wrung Mikah's hand without knowing he did. Mikah's bow clattered onto the boards, and he would have dropped the violin next, but one of the officers spoke.

"You, fiddler, play something. Play for dancing."

He could have said *play for the fish about to rain from the sky*; Mikah found the chinrest somewhere near his chin. Fayge, her face still painted, bent in the slow silent way of someone who wishes not to be shot, and handed him his bow.

"Anything," she begged him, behind the falling gold of her hair. "Hirsh, tell him to play . . . "

"Aren't you hungry, Jews?"

"Of course they're hungry. Think we've poisoned it."

"It's your opening night. Don't you want your little party? Go on, it's for you, a party!" The man spoke to children, or

44

dogs, throwing bits of Yiddish into his speech and laughing, much too heartily, in the face of all their weariness and fear.

"Ungrateful goddamned monkeys! Eat! Drink! Dance!"

They stood still, all of them, in the heavy heat of their ill-fitting costumes, dripping sweat and makeup under the lights. Not even Leyb, who spent his days smuggling his weight in potatoes and onions, stirred toward the feast.

One of the officers, who had not spoken, suddenly moved. He was neat, flawlessly silver and black; he was one of the officers who had not crossed into the Ghetto proper since the bloody fiery days before its birth. "Play a waltz!"

He grabbed Fayge and held her to him.

Beniek shouted, and it took Hirsh and Violeta bracing hard to hold him. Fayge had her eyes closed and her mouth shut. Mikah swallowed harsh sourness. He played.

"Here's to your opening night!"

"Here's to a little fun, little Jews!"

From the spray that dashed against his cheek, Hirsh knew the Germans had gotten to the champagne. He took his glasses off and polished them, and polished them.

"Do something," someone hissed in his ear, so close the warmth was uncomfortable. "Get her away from him, cut in on their dance, I don't care, before Beniek kills one of them."

"Cut in? Are you mad?"

Raissa was beside him. "Course I'm mad. Stark raving."

"I'll get killed!"

"We all might, if Vi can't hold him!" Raissa glared, with her head on one side, birdlike; then she muttered, "oh *here*, for fuck's sake, hold my glasses." She was bright-pale under the hot lights, in her dark vest and trousers. Hirsh bit the inside of his cheek and watched her go. Maybe she did cut into the waltz, and maybe she didn't; there was a sound, a body's weight of flesh striking wood, and then Fayge and the officer were no longer dancing. Everyone noticed nothing, very studiously, and the choir, under orders, began to sing *Tum Balalaika*.

[October 1941]

"Read this," Hirsh said. "You have a better German than I."

Raissa frowned at the Gothic print. "I don't know why they don't print these in the vernacular."

"Maybe they do it for fun," said Sheyndl. "What's it say, Rais'le?"

"They're opening up the public baths on Jerozolim Street." Raissa whistled, incredulous.

"Why? What for?" Hirsh had thrown himself across the stage with Raissa's black cardigan under his head, but he sat up to avoid glimpsing Fayge's legs beneath her skirt.

"They say they want to stop the epidemic."

"Oh, why, when it's rolling so merrily along? Six streets they've got quarantined off, how will those people get to the baths?"

"A public bath in January, people will freeze!"

"It could be a trap."

"Who cares if it's a trap?" Raissa leaned back in her chair, groaning bliss. "Hot water! Soap!"

"You've got soap? Not me."

"Not me either." The chair's feet thumped the floor.

"It isn't a trap." Fayge shrugged. "It's in their best interest. They drink from the same wells. They die just like us."

"A toast to typhus, then," Raissa grinned. "To fevers! To rashes! To spots!"

"To people dying," Hirsh quenched her.

"We've all had the typhus. There's no harm in it, if we do go. And it's a bath."

"I haven't," Raissa said. "But I don't mean to die of spots."

"It's the trouble with you high-quality people. Better you were born someplace nice and dirty, a one-room over the tannery maybe, and got it all over with as children, like us."

"Hirsh, we were all born in the Levite hospital, and you got every vaccine there is." Sheyndl looked reproachfully at him.

"Otherwise a strong wind would have killed him."

"It didn't, more's the pity, I'm sure. But I still don't have any soap."

Fayge went to her coat, crumpled in the wings, and dug for a moment in the lining. She came back with a handful of tiny, paper-wrapped hotel soaps. "These all right?"

"These are from the Hotel Pannonia," Sheyndl gaped. "I know the double-eagle on the front."

"Closest to the Hotel Pannonia we'll ever be," gloated Raissa, pressing the soap to her nose and inhaling its perfume.

"It was all right," Fayge replied. "The food was nothing to write home about."

"What? You've been in there? But it's been closed to Jews and dogs since nineteen-thirty-three . . . "

"Tell us what it was like," Sheyndl broke in. "Tell us what you ate!"

"Tell us how you got in and who you were with," Raissa said, bitterly. "Did my brother know? Now there's a story to entertain the kiddies."

Quick as a shock, Fayge slapped her.

Hirsh got to his feet, slowly. "Thank you for the soap," he said. "We all thank you. And maybe Raissa's will get somewhere near her mouth."

"Maybe it'll choke her," said Fayge. "No, keep it, use it. I should feel sorry for you, the way you cough up your life. How long did they tell you at the infirmary, three months, four?"

"I'd rather cough up my life than—"

Hirsh stepped between them, trembling with nerves.

"Please, no more fighting. If nothing else, we're supposed to go and get tickets by noon for the, er, for the public bath."

The showers worked, and they were hot. Five at a time, men, women, children together, the Jewish Police let them in to the old ritual baths; and there was green slime across the floors, the mikvah pools were empty and algae-brown, but the water was running and the line for a bath ticket went around the block.

Hirsh had forgotten there were still children in the Ghetto to get dirty. He had forgotten the feeling of a shower, public or private, the sluicing water, the comfort of soap. His mouth dried with the thought of so much water, and he wondered what Mikah would say. He had taken to wearing a black ribbon on his armband, for Mikah, the way Raissa wore one for Violeta. Alive, maybe, but not close enough to see or touch, and so more dead than the real dead, as far as the Ghetto was concerned. Those typhoid-rashy people stacked on the carts so near the bathhouse, they weren't dead, just catching a lucky snooze on the Germans' time. A loved one disappeared, resettled, Hirsh had learned to mourn for that; because in the not-knowing, the not-death, there was hope and hope could keep the pain fresh.

The pain lived behind his ribs, where a thin invisible cord connected him to his twin. In broad daylight, queuing with five hundred other people and clutching his little soaplet, he mourned and Mikah would not go away.

With Raissa and Sheyndl and two strangers he was let into the bathhouse, fast, at a run, as it was with everything else. He had not learned, like Raissa, to strip with a hand or a foot always tight on his discarded clothes; his necktie and vest were gone before he knew it, but the water was still ahead, clean and warm as a promise.

He realized slowly that Raissa was naked, an armful of black clothing bundled out of the way, her black hair falling across her breasts. Nothing at all hid the harsh slant of her ribs, or anything below it.

He stared, until she splashed him, and then he colored to the ears.

"Take a picture, Hirshke," she called to him, and when he looked up, she flicked the wet stranded hair from her breasts. He got more than an idea of her nipples, then, though long starvation had changed her, made all her soft lines more cruel; he could fill in his mind's sketch of the shape of her.

She turned her back, laughing, just before he had to hold his balled-up shirt against his waist.

"For God's sake, Hirshke, I don't care if you look at me!"

"Don't look at me," he half echoed, half begged, and knew she couldn't hear. This was not how he had ever imagined being naked with her, with three other people and in a hurry and with soap streaming into his eyes. He drew his lower lip hard against his teeth, and stayed silent. Raissa did not speak to him again, even when they had left the showers and dried themselves, miserably, on their clothing; if she noticed his shirt was soaked, her eyes never let it show.

[January 1942]

"In Warsaw there's a committee, they're writing everything down, for, you know. For the end." Hirsh looked slightly wistful. "Plays. Poetry. Diaries."

"How do they intend to preserve all of it?"

"How do they know the words might survive, if they don't?"

"Wait, you said—Warsaw, how do you know from Warsaw?"

"I had a letter from my cousin." Under the questioning gazes Hirsh turned slightly pinker around the pallor, and became interested in the bitten-thin tips of his fingernails.

"And what have you had since?"

Hirsh stirred his spoon around the empty curve of his bowl as if to conjure more soup.

"It's still a good idea, Hirshke," Raissa said. "But such a risk, that's all we're saying. Think of what we'd be signing our names to, is all."

"You never used to care about risks. Now, what's the matter now, no more big brother to buy you out of trouble?"

"Shut up about my brother," she said. What came next was lost in a gust of coughing, a quick startled struggle for air, and though she folded her handkerchief small into her hand, everyone in the café could have seen the red.

Fayge curved a protective hand over her daughter's face, heedless of the damp, sticky bread that fell on her skirt, and the protesting cry that followed. Sheyndl scrooged down smaller on her side of the booth.

"What? I'm all right."

Hirsh pushed his water glass towards her, conciliatory. "I didn't mean, Rais'le—" he started.

"Never mind." She gulped all of his water and half his cup of tea, and found a deep breath. "It does violate a direct order. It's death, you know, to write it all down. Not a camp somewhere, just a nice walk up the hill and a bullet in the head."

"Where would we keep it, how would we keep it, if we did? Paper rots in the ground," Sheyndl ventured.

"How should I know how we'll keep it? None of that matters if we don't write it!"

"Hirshke . . . "

Fayge's hand came down on the table between them. "Write your book," she said. "Don't worry about the rest." She gathered Mir'ele against her shoulder, fished up a handful of Reichsmark bills, and rose from the table. "I think you're all crazy, you know, you Easterners," she was calling, over her shoulder, before Hirsh could hurry the waiter for her change.

Drums, he dreamed of drums. Gunshots, maybe, or hail, or . . .

A handful of wet gravel made it through the window and onto his face. Spluttering, Hirsh sat up and groped for his eyeglasses. There was no more candle left in the candle-holder, but the moon hung close and brilliant over the snowy courtyard. Below the window someone small, shrouded, breathed their impatience in heavy clouds.

"Hirsh!"

Dim and worn and fluttering on the chilly wind, he saw the yellow flags for typhoid and the red for scarlatina, out on the rickety balconies, and knew why she did not come up. He buttoned his coat on over his shirt, with only a second's hesitation when he buttoned the two accidentally together, and took the stairs down into the courtyard three at a time.

"Fayge? I mean, Mrs. Gellerman? What on earth can I do for you?"

"Leave your armband," she ordered, the whisper somehow carrying above all the other night noises. Hirsh flinched.

"Leave it, and come with me."

"But what—I mean where—"

"To see your brother."

He followed her. His death waited in every shadow, at the blind corner of every street, and he followed her. She was a shadow, quick and quiet, just another part of the night; he felt like the clanging, clamoring rusty tin can at her heels. Somewhere not too near there were dogs barking, their leashes jingling to the tramp, tramp of their handler's heels in the snow. As they neared the wire, there were sudden great blazes of light, and she had to haul him sharply backward, into the dark again.

"Wait for me," hissed Fayge, "or be killed, for all I care!"

Mikah's face seemed to peer out at him, a wraith their two breaths made. She could have been leading him to the river or to the moon. He followed her.

"Still," she ordered, behind a building that backed onto the wire itself. He waited, as still as he could be with his teeth clattering in the cold and his knees shuddering from fear; she went to the wire. She touched it. She lifted a rusty section of it free.

There was a gap, bright pearl-cold night, in the wire. There was freedom as high as his head, spanning maybe the breadth of his two hands. Fayge beckoned to him then, and somehow he moved, he was walking, to the wire, to his death.

He was through the wire, and her hand was in his and they ran, heedless of snow and of shoes, breath smarting. He felt her heart, through her hand. They ran like hell.

Sparks were floating on his vision, when Fayge stopped them. Hirsh looked up, startled, and found himself on St. Joseph's street. At the top of the hill was the old yeshiva, and at the bottom of the hill, his home.

"My God, how did we get here?"

"Stop speaking Yiddish, and put your arm around me. Quick."

Walking like that, slowed by the drifts on the sidewalk, Hirsh had time to look in the shop windows they passed. There was the barber and the fruiterer's and what had been Berkowitz's delicatessen, still with its rolled-down tin shutter and the pickle barrels guarding the door, but not Berkowitz's anymore. The sky was clear, and the air had the faint sweetness of wood smoke. Snow fell, lazily, in tiny spirals, and Hirsh breathed and felt free.

"My brother? He's alive? He's all right?"

"Stow your fucking Yiddish," Fayge said, pulling him into a doorway, as if for a kiss. Her brows were drawn into a forbidding line, and her eyes held fire. "I am not going to get killed tonight. I've decided already. Now shut up, please, unless you can speak without that accent."

Hirsh nodded, then shook his head, to show he understood, and he couldn't.

"Speak French to me, I've heard you speak French. I don't care if you say *banana, banana.*"

"Say what?"

"Oh, God. Save me."

"What's a—"

She had stepped down from the doorway and he had no choice but to escort her, or follow her, where she led. Up the hill and further up, into the leaning old heart of the city, where the buildings were all strange dark brick and river stone; past the convent and the cathedral, and round about and back again, by the corner of the empty market square, and finally to a place where no streetlights burned, where all the windows were boarded and the doorways loomed like empty mouths.

"Romm's," Hirsh whispered, high and thin with surprise. "My brother—"

"Get in, you idiot."

There was no light. He followed her, touching her shoulder, and he thought his eyes would adjust but it only seemed to get darker. It had been a printing house, for hundreds of years, before the occupation. A hundred or so years of darkness pressed on Hirsh's eyes now, as if some god's hand was spilling a constant soft stream of black ink. Enough to ink Talmuds, enough to enliven Aleichem till Chelm sprang up off the page, enough to make him crash his knees into a press and cry out.

"Breyder'le," someone said, quietly, and there was a candle.

"Mikah!"

"Sorry for the darkness. There have been people in the neighborhood," Mikah explained. "More than there should be."

Fayge looked askance at the street, behind them, but all Hirsh saw was Mikah. He was paler, unshaven, and cold reddened his cheeks and nose. He wore a cut-down Russian army coat, and there was a rifle in a sling across his back. He was thin as a rail and smiling.

"Look at you. A gentleman. My brother."

"Mikah," Hirsh said, and repeated it, maybe. He was holding his twin, hard, around the shoulders and the middle as if he might disappear.

"Come upstairs, Hirshke, and look at your book."

"There isn't time," Fayge interjected. "I'll never get him across in daylight."

"I can stay here, with him," Hirsh began.

"No." Two voices, at once. Mikah, still smiling, knocked a tear off his cheek. "Brother, you can't stay here. We can't stay here. Been too long in one place. But it's done now," he added. "Fifty copies. All inked by hand."

"All in the bloody dark." Someone was coming, very slowly, tread by tread down the stairs. By voice he recognized Avrom, the postmaster's son; he could not tear his eyes from Mikah.

Fayge, near them, was taking off her coat in spite of the cold. Dimly Hirsh heard the sound of objects falling, shifting, and an absurdly bright sardine tin caught the candlelight for a second.

"Gourmet dining," said Mikah. "Our last meal in this place, God willing. We're going out to the frontier in an hour."

"The frontier," Hirsh mouthed, trying to understand. "You're leaving."

"We only came into the city to print the book." Mikah

disengaged from the embrace, gently.

"The book?"

"*Lider un Poemes fun der Geto Vilna*," Mikah nodded, when Hirsh babbled soundlessly as a fish. "The first work from Don't Let the Bastards Shoot Us printing house. Catchy little name, don't you think?"

"Our book, you printed our book, I—I don't care about the book!"

"I do," said Mikah. "I'm in it."

"But you're alive," Hirsh managed. "And you won't—you're not coming back with us."

"No."

Hirsh held on to his brother's arms, when he would have fallen.

"We have to go," Fayge murmured, kindly as Hirsh had ever heard her speak. "It's half five. There's no more time."

"Go carefully," said Avrom. "It's been too busy around here."

"Go quickly and carefully." Mikah kissed his twin, once, on the forehead. "Trust Fayge. She's a good guide."

"Mikah . . . "

"Hirsh." And Mikah turned his back, because there was no time to say anything else, nothing more to say, and he could not watch his brother go.

Fayge led him down the steps of the printing house, her delicate arm strong when he stumbled. She led him, like a blind man, through the streets where a murky kind of dawn was rising from the snowdrifts; she led him to the wire and held it, though he caught his hand anyway, snagged the skin and it bled. Her raincoat was stiff and heavy with books, fifty pieces of bound-paper armor in its lining; Hirsh took off his own coat and offered it to her. He could not, honestly, feel any more of the cold.

She was speaking to him, refusing his coat, low and gently as if she spoke to her child, and she had tied her handkerchief around his hand, somehow. He had been looking at the start of the sunrise, a red streak along the gray at the river's edge, and he never felt a thing. From a pocket she dredged two armbands, torn, wrinkled; they were Jews again, inside again, and Mikah was out there. Hirsh wanted to cry, or kiss her for leading him, or curse her for letting Mikah stay behind.

They had turned their backs on the wire, and headed down the hill, when the ground shook and the sky roared. Black smoke plumed into the winter dawn-dark, and bricks struck the snow around them and hissed with heat.

Fayge dove for cover, hauling him with her half by accident. The smoke was still rolling, following the wind, and it had spread to the onion dome of St. Kazimier.

"What happened?" Hirsh spat out grit.

"About twenty depth charges happened," said Fayge. "They blew a building down."

Hirsh sat down in the snow.

"Hirsh!"

"My brother," he managed to make her understand, even though she didn't, quite.

[February 1942]

II.

She is leaving the house where she was born. She leaves behind books, silvered mirrors, a box of chocolates half eaten. She leaves her horse and her chambermaid and all her stake in the bank. She has money, a little, three thousand zloty in a silk handkerchief; it's going to have to do. It's hers from Loniek, her favorite brother, no one can say she stole it.

Down the corridor he sleeps, and she will never see him again.

She is seventeen-years-old and finished school, this June, but she will not stay to graduate. She will not stay on this side of the river a moment longer. Her sisters, who have scorned her since she put away her skirts, swear to slaughter her if she steps foot in the street and brings them scandal; her brothers, but for Loniek, no longer speak to her at all. It would be different if Beniek was not so far away: Beniek who could stand against Father and win. But he had been a grown man almost when she was born, and now he was in Venice, Paris, somewhere. For Purim he had sent her a crimson necktie and crimson enamel cufflinks, in a haberdashery box marked in gilt in French.

The necktie's gone, she is certain, but Father never

thought to look for cufflinks. She puts them in her coat pocket now, in the half-dark towards morning, and tries not to think of Purim.

There was a party, there always had been, though it was too cold to dance in the garden. Raissa, allowed two guests of her own, had chosen Sheyndl Berkowitz and Violeta; Sheyndl was a butterfly, in wings of her own design, and Violeta was the Tsarevna Anastasia, very wry, but Raissa had gone as a boy. Just a boy, in a collar and tie and one of Marek's tail-coats, cut down. The best of Vilna was at that party, and no one whispered yet that the Gellerman girl was unnatural. She was just a young thing in a costume, playing in the shadow of her brothers.

There had been wine, and Violeta. Raissa had learnt to waltz from her sisters' dancing-master, though it was a hard thing to do backwards, and they had made three turns around the upstairs hallway before the wine got into Raissa's brain. The rest of the night, she was less sure of; there was a kiss, she knew, hands and the yielding edge of a bed, skin and the fine red of Violeta's hair. Violeta was older, protesting, prudent, but Raissa was spoiled and fearless, skilled at winning her own way. *This is my home,* she'd whispered, *where are we safe, if not here?*

But the house was old, and all the upstairs doors opened to one key. It must have been three in the morning, or past, and they were asleep when Ania came knocking. And then she tired of knocking, before Raissa could find her shirt. Ania flung the door wide into their darkness; that odious fish-monger girl had fallen asleep on the downstairs chaise, and would Raissa kindly come and rouse—

Her sister's scream—a high and perfect scream, and Raissa will remember it—brought all three brothers. Half-drunk, half-costumed, half-asleep, Marek and Lysiek reached them first. Loniek was behind, a little winded from the servants' stairs. He shouted, when Lysiek took one of Violeta's arms and Marek the other, but he was too late to do anything but shout. Raissa had pleaded with him to go after them, before they hurt Violeta, but he had stayed behind. Loniek found clothes for her, a skirt from the back of the wardrobe, shoes, a ribbon to bind back her hair. She did not remember if he had spoken to her, did not recall hearing his voice again at all until she was crouched, near fainting, on the library carpet in front of their father. Blood was slipping down her back and she thought she would fall into the fire, and Loniek was there, crying at Father to look what he'd done, *for God's pity, she's the youngest.* Then Loniek had picked her up, and she really had fainted . . .

The marks have faded to briar-scratches beneath her shirt; the linen no longer catches when she moves. Her fingers are cold as, by the cold candle, she finishes dressing. She will leave by the front door, since the dogs are down in the kitchen garden, across the bridge and down into the Jewish quarter on foot, not more than half an hour's run.

If Loniek comes after her, she will not know what to say.

She leaves the house, leaves her brothers, leaves the life that stretches false and stifling before her sight. She makes nimble time, it's downhill and she can have no fear, even of the dark, while running. Before the pack has grown heavy on her shoulders, she stands before the door she wanted to find. The courtyard is silent, no one in the building yet stirs, but she has the key.

Home.

THE GRAVES GROWING HERE

" . . . the single road leads to Ponar,
with no road leading back . . . "
— A. Volkoviski

There were four glasses of tea on the café table, four lumps of
sugar and four transparent slices of lemon; only two of the
chairs were occupied. Fayge flicked at her wristwatch, left
her tea settling, and paid attention only to the door.

"They say Siauliai will rise."

"Siauliai?" Fayge repeated. "Peasants."

"But—"

"If they had the strength to do it, their children would
never have been taken away." Fayge's lips turned at one
corner, but it was not a smile. "Six thousand children onto
the trains? Herr Glik, I think the shooting would start." She
held her daughter in her lap, and went on feeding grapes to
the soundless child; there was a smear of red around the
mouth that had never, in Hirsh's sight, formed a word or
even cried.

"Kovno then. If we fight, so will Kovno!"

"A little louder, please, for the dish-boys who didn't hear
you." Fayge glared him into flushed stillness. But it was one

o'clock and the café was full; cutlery clinked, chairs screeched across the marble floors, and over the door a bright bell wagged. No one looked up from their food.

"Where is my husband? Where the hell is Raissa?"

"I'm late, of course. Are those grapes?" Raissa, in black with her black hair falling unchecked, leaned across Hirsh to reach for the bowl.

"No," said Fayge, cool.

"Oh, come on, just one!" Raissa turned a chair backward and sat with her chin propped, staring at their frost-touched purple.

"I've ordered cutlets, for you and for Beni. Keep your pestilent paws away."

"Perfectly clean!" Raissa protested. "Beniek's not coming. Can't come. And I can't get in to see him, either." Her armband had fallen past her elbow, and she hitched it to its proper place on her rusty-black sleeve. The black ribbon she'd sewn along the armband's edge had bled, in snow and rain, to strange blue. "They say he's with the Council, in committee. They're turning all the wives away at the door."

"Were you hurt?" Hirsh asked, a frown deepening as he cut Raissa's portion of heavy dark bread.

"Not to notice. I can butter it myself, Hirshke."

"Of course you can, and with my share of it besides." He did not relinquish the butter-knife. "I'm not worried. God knows they've sat around talking before."

"I'm worried," Raissa disagreed. "Ah! Food!"

The cutlets, beef or horse, stilled all noise at their table; it was some quarter of an hour before Fayge set down her knife and fork, dabbed her lips on her handkerchief and said, "Why?"

"Why who?" Raissa, still chewing, managed to slip half her meat onto Hirsh's plate; he countered with a boiled potato, and she stuck her fork into his forearm. "You need it more, I'm smaller."

"You're sick," he said.

"So, I eat like an invalid. I'm making perfect sense. Why, what?" she repeated.

"Why are you worried?" Fayge shifted her daughter's weight, to give Mir'ele sips from her water glass. "I never knew you to take your head out of a book so long."

"It's been quiet at night," Raissa replied. "Really quiet. You don't hear the trucks. They're not taking anyone away."

"Thank God."

"No, Hirshke, listen. Sheyndl's work permit expired two weeks ago."

"So . . . ?"

"She's still here."

"Thank God, I said already."

"I will when I see Him," Raissa snapped. "No one in Ghetto B has valid permits, not since first January. That must be seven thousand people. Alive. Not working."

Fayge nodded, slow as sunrise. Hirsh's tea glass hovered an inch from his chin, until Raissa put out a hand to lower it.

"So what are they waiting for?"

[December 1941]

"At six o'clock this evening, the ghetto is hermetically sealed," Beniek read aloud, and his voice was almost without panic. "Everyone who is alive should report to the Dzielna market, under pain of death."

"I never understood that one," Raissa called, into the thickening dread. Her voice was jackdaw-rough and she perched in the one chair, uneasy. "Are we meant to fear the pain part, or the death?"

"Sha," said someone. Everyone had come to the theatre

after the last round of soup to be got out of the public kitchen, though there was no call that evening. Sheyndl stood braiding and re-braiding a length of her chestnut hair, and was shrill.

"Herr Direktor, please, what do we do?"

Beniek looked startled. He was the oldest among them, and the Judenrat had kept him late, weeks on end now, in council; he would know. He would know what none of them knew; but he looked around at the tight miserable circle of them, buttoning gloves or fixing bootlaces or tossing *Passiert* wallets from hand to hand, and his mouth stayed an inch open and silent.

Fayge came in then. Her stockings were straight, and her bright hair was rolled and pinned under her hat. The hat's feather was stuck in her lapel, for safekeeping. She walked quietly forward, into the gloom, as if it slid off her. Beniek crossed to her in a stride, took her arms at the elbows. They might have been about to kiss.

"Where have you been? Where is Mir'ele?"

"Safe."

"She—" Beniek swallowed all but a whisper. "I will not have our daughter at risk in a melina somewhere!"

"No melina," Fayge agreed. "Safe."

"Where—"

"You think I would have left her in a coal cellar, under floorboards? For them to find!"

Raissa's hand on Beniek's sleeve stopped them. "Be still," she begged. "They look at you, they all look at you . . . " She slid a glance back for Mendel and Talia, his wife the contralto who was nineteen and had gray eyes and a smile like pearl. She had no more bread than any of them, and no winter shoes, but Mendel's hand was on her shoulder and she was seven months gone with child.

"Breyderl, tell them what to do."

He let go of both of them, and faced the eighteen or nineteen people who had never stood anyplace like this before. "It will be a bad night," Beniek said finally, rusty. "If you know a place to hide, go there. Go now. It is twenty-four minutes to six."

"Is that all?" Hirsh's eyes had the fixed look of diamonds. His voice came piping. "You're on the inside, every day, and that's all you can tell us?"

"If you're going to hide, don't be taken alive," Beniek added, straight to him. "It's seleckja; we've lived through seleckja before. I have no idea what it's for, or what they will be thinking. Do you think they tell us?"

"I think they tell you more than—"

"More than any man would want to know."

"How many will they take? How many do they want?"

"Seven thousand, no more," Beniek replied, to Geza the first clarinet or Moishe the second, and he was looking at a knot in the stage, so that Raissa knew it for a lie.

"And what happens to the ones they take?"

"Work in the East," answered Beniek. "Resettlement."

"In the East," Sheyndl repeated. "What's east of here?"

Hirsh snapped, "Nothing, nowhere; he's doing as he's been told." He unfolded from the desktop where he had been sitting, doodling with a wax pencil on what had once been set design, or blocking, and now no longer mattered because tomorrow night, the number of players would not be the same. "What's east of here, Sheyndl, little one, but Ponar?"

Sheyndl wailed, and Raissa would have slapped him, but he was moving too fast away from them all, out the door. It scraped and clanged behind him, sharp as the end of a dream.

"Sheyndl, it's all right, sha, sha, sha . . . trust my brother, trust Herr Gens. Herr Gens is very clever, he won't let anything happen to us."

"I've—I've never met Herr Gens!"

"Yes, you have. He taught the boys, remember? Sucked on sugared almonds all the time, always icing around his mouth?"

"You think he'll remember us?"

"He knows who we are." Raissa grinned. "Go on, let go."

"You are a better liar than your brother," Fayge murmured when Raissa straightened up. "You wouldn't know Jakob Gens if he kissed you on the mouth."

Raissa backed away, startled. "Neither would you."

"That's why my faith is elsewhere." Fayge gave a very refined shrug that seemed to move everything from coat-buttons to eyebrows in its indifference. "By the way, he's a diabetic."

The theatre had emptied, while they whispered back and forth; Beniek stood in his muffler, hatless, waiting to put out the candles. Maybe he was nervous, but his back was straight and his expression stilled. He had a clean armband half unfolded on the desk, and with his penknife he trimmed the ties. Raissa remembered to fish for her crumpled one, and found it in the pocket of her water-stained tawny leather jacket.

"Raissa, what about you?" Beniek said it when she moved, as if it had not crossed his mind before.

"What about me? You're going to Dzielna, aren't you? I'll walk with you. There's only time to go straight there."

"But you—you can't—"

"I'll go in the lines with everyone else. I'm not going to hide."

"You've shown more sense before—with Violeta—"

"Violeta is gone," said Raissa, and shrugged on her jacket.

It was a beautiful dusk. The sky over the river was shell-purple, darkening around the stars. No snow fell. The streets were strange, quiet, clear of all things, even the dead. The loudest sound was the slip-slish of Raissa's boots over the road. Fayge, she noted, had excellent boots, black leather banded with sealskin. Their tops disappeared beneath the muddy hem of her raincoat, and they made her ankles look well-turned indeed; and Beniek could not have afforded them for his wife.

She would have remarked, but they came up onto level ground, to the marketplace, and the light knocked away all her thought. Bright as day, Dzielna Square was lit by great electric lanterns, and at one corner the Jewish Police had a bonfire going. There were no dark corners to hide in. No shadows lay across the snow. Glittering-white and painful to the eyes, the Square was already half filled with people. They were the ones who had faced all this before, who did not want to be driven from their ragged homes into the dark, or who preferred to know where and when the bullet would find them. They would all stand for hours, turning to ice, while the stragglers were roused, while the screaming rose. Raissa had never borne a real *seleckja*, and to her it did not seem, yet, like such a terrible thing. An endless time spent standing, waiting; everyone was used to that. Her head was beginning to ache from the cold.

"Breyderl," she murmured, "what's going to happen?"

There was thunder, before he could answer. When lightning flared, some near them began to cry that it was the Messiah, a sign . . . Raissa jumped, wild-eyed, though it was so bright in the Square that even lightning could not really dazzle. Fayge shrugged deeper into her raincoat, and Beniek put an arm around her shoulders. Then all was still again. Breathing; coughing; but no one spoke.

"Beniek—"

"Stay with Fayge," Beniek said, and nothing else.

It rained. Sharp with bits of ice, turning the snow into slush-pools around their feet: it came down like cold knives. It was too early in the year for rain. Under the open sky, everyone pressed closer together by instinct; though the market was not full, Raissa could suddenly feel Fayge shivering hard against her side, and strangers were treading on her toes and her heels. Rainwater froze in her hair, biting at her fingers when she tucked it back. The air she breathed rasped through her, cold and wet.

Drenched, dripping, they waited. Fayge, who had gloves, fumbled her watch out into the open, and it was half until eight.

"Please," she said, to no one, in German. "I'm cold!"

It was half until nine.

Raissa had bitten her lips together, and blood tinged the warmth around her tongue. Beniek stood staring out into the brilliant night, and Fayge had fainted, it seemed, standing only because the crush of people forced her. She was nowhere the touch of Raissa's hand—even warm, a little, and dry from the shelter of her jacket—could reach her.

Around the three of them, Dzielna Square had at last filled: men in worn wet caps, and women in draggled hats, all looking the same shade of brown-black under the terrible light. If they talked, it went unheard in the rain; if they had been hurt, there was no room to turn and see the marks. Surely by now the snatchers were out, with their whips and their dogs; certainly it would start soon, whatever was going to start.

It was ten o'clock.

Behind them, somewhere, Raissa could hear rough shouts, even with her ears washed numb by the rain. There was gunfire, automatic, strident. Fayge came back to herself, gasping, and caught at Raissa's arm.

"It's just noise," Fayge said, after a moment, and very carefully took her hand away.

"Good evening, Jews!"

Some screamed, and Beniek bowed his head, but Fayge made a swift two-fingered gesture.

"I hope you have all passed a pleasant few hours!"

Squinting through the rain, and rising as far on her toes as worn-out boots would allow, Raissa made out the speaker. He was on horseback, in a mackintosh that gleamed with rain; all black, all black, but for his face, and he held his black horse to near stillness, though the crowd and the weather had maddened it.

"Murer," said Fayge, for Raissa's benefit. "Leutnant-Gebietskommissar."

"He's what?"

"He's the devil," Fayge replied. "You're taller, is there another? A man with him. The horse is silver, with a white blaze. Is there another?"

Beniek turned, at the frantic note in her whispers, and pulled Fayge into his arms, though it jostled bodies in all directions. An elbow jabbed into Raissa's back, and she nearly folded like a pocketknife. Murer was speaking again, when the pain passed; he shouted orders in plain bare German, the way one called to a wayward child or dog, and then the air was filled with the *click, snap, click* of rifles brought forward and primed.

"Breyderl!" Raissa called out, in panic.

It was not Beniek who answered her. Fayge slipped from her husband's arms. "Don't take out your papers, not unless they order it. Try and stay to the right."

"Form columns, you idiot Jews, unless you like the rain! Men to the left, women to the right!"

The mass of them, ten thousand people, tried to move at once: quickly enough to obey the order, not so quickly as to be shot. Raissa caught at anyone, anything, before she stumbled, and someone braced her at the shoulder.

"Don't fall. If you go down, they'll shoot."

" . . . Fayge?"

"Don't fall."

She could not turn, right or any direction; the crush was too great, and too close. The air was sharp with powder-smoke. Ahead of her there was a gap, and she was carried towards it, much too fast. She reached out; her hand closed on a stranger's rags.

"Beniek! Beniek! Beniek!"

He caught her around the chest, a second before she would have been dragged down. Raissa stopped scrabbling and turned to him. Her brother's coat was torn, and his hands were bleeding. He was distracted, his eyes held no attention, even for his sister and his wife. By the blaze of rifle-muzzles, bright on bright, Raissa made out Fayge; her golden hair stood out in the rain, even among so many people.

A tremendous pull on her shoulder, then. Pain enough to make her fall into the freezing water round Beniek's feet, pain that curled her into a knot, and when she opened her eyes all the could see was boots, black, gleaming.

"Men to the left! Women to the right!" A gust of schnapps and onion and rotten teeth. Cold water and tears blinded her, but she saw the rifle-butt meant for her hit Fayge, saw Beniek's face as Fayge pitched into the mud. Around her, shouting, voices and faces she knew, and the fear, the cold and the rain. They were shouting to Beniek, above her, trying to calm him, to stop him from—

Fayge.

Face-down in three inches of water in the street, and stunned.

Raissa found her own feet, somehow, and two inches from a gun's mouth she was completely ignored. Someone was coming through the rain.

"You goatfucking sons of dirt, that's my singer!" Murer, down from his horse, mackintosh flying wide to show a brace of pistols; Raissa gibbered in terror, and the Jewish Police did the same. He struck out with his fists, snarling curses faster than Raissa could translate. Then he went to one knee in the icy mud, and helped Fayge upright.

"What are you doing here?" He was not shouting, and around them the madness was no less, but Raissa heard it. Fayge, scraped, blue-lipped and choking, seemed to hang in his arms for a moment.

"Go! Get out of here! Disappear!" Murer flung her away. "Disappear!"

Fayge grabbed Raissa's arm, and followed orders. They ran until she fell, tumbling between the street and the gutter, with Raissa skidding on the ice behind her. She picked herself up with a wince, and a limp that stayed when they ran on. They ran blind on treacherous winter streets, but neither would look back to the light in the market square.

For a long time, they strained the silence only by their breathing. Raissa could not see her watch-face, except by the white bursts that meant the shooting was too near; but there was time enough for the stitch in her ribs to dissolve, and the pain in her back and shoulders settled unremarkable as a metronome.

Fayge sat in the crook of two buildings, heedless of the rain that pooled and puddled. Her hair was slapped in dull strings down her neck, rain dripped from her nose and lashes, every layer of clothing was drenched and her hat and gloves were gone. She steepled her fingers around her nose for a moment and blew into them, to warm them; then she took off her armband, tested the wet canvas with a stretch, and used it to bind up her ankle.

"What are we doing out here?" Raissa asked, crouching to be heard.

"Hiding, I thought."

"In the middle of the avenue! Under the sky!"

"Sky like this, they won't pay any heed to what's out beneath it." Fayge winced.

"My brother told me to take care of you."

"I don't need taking care of."

There was so much in the words that Raissa swallowed and blinked and moved over them. "Do you think Beniek's all right?"

"He's with Gens. He's all right."

"I thought he would kill that man, the one who had hold of you—"

"Beniek has more sense than that."

"You were hurt. You were down in the mud; you didn't see his face. It took Yurek Posner *and* Herr Gutgestalt to hold him."

"If he had touched one of them, Raissa, we all would have died. He knows—Beniek knows when he can do nothing," she finished, somewhat lamely. She tipped her head back and listened, to something Raissa could not distinguish from the thick fusillade. "And I'm not hurt."

She squinted into the rain and the dark, and Raissa followed her eyes, though the rain drove harder than ever and freezing.

"What is it?"

"Headlights," replied Fayge. She could not have gotten paler, but by her expression and her wide blue eyes she blanched. "We have to get away from here."

"I thought—"

"Move!"

Raissa was too water-blinded to see Fayge get up, but the young woman's weight full against her back pitched her over the closest dark threshold. Before the war, the building had been a guesthouse; there was a concierge's booth, a double staircase, and the black-on-darkness hint of doorways and large spaces beyond. Raissa crashed into the stairs, and skinned her palms on a row of carpet tacks; someone had long since stolen the carpet.

"I thought you said we were better off being still . . . "

"Not anymore." Fayge had found, half by touch, the porter's door into the courtyard behind the building. She put her shoulder to it and pushed, and they were on the New Alley, out of sight of the market square and the main roads. Raissa could get no useful bearings, for a moment; it took her that long to realize that overhead was an electric streetlight, and it worked.

"Come on!" Fayge flattened, out of the light. She was limping, and the alley was not well-paved, but she was the faster.

"Where the hell are we going?"

"Anywhere!"

"Not that way, it goes too close to the trains!"

Fayge checked, at the turning of the alley. She stared out as if cattle cars waited no further away than the nearest crumbling arch. "Left then."

"And be back at Dzielna! Sure, why not, at least my brother's there!"

They crossed the gutters and walked straight ahead, because there was nowhere else.

"Why were we running?"

"You wanted to go on that truck, have a nice evening drive to Ponar?"

"It's getting light, don't you think?" Raissa replied with a question.

"I don't think," Fayge hissed back.

"But the shooting's less . . . "

"That only means they're farther into the schnapps. How can we be lost? You've lived here all your life!"

"Not in the dark," answered Raissa. "Not without my brothers."

They picked and threaded their way, mostly quiet because Fayge's teeth had started to chatter, across the larger ghetto. It was the small ghetto's turn, now, to be lit in terrible bursts, and fragmented by screams.

"D-do you have any, I mean, family?"

"My parents are dead," said Fayge, very steadily. "I had—I have—someone like a sister. In Vienna. I think I would know, if she—if Alma was no longer alive."

"What is she like?"

"I don't know." In profile Fayge seemed to frown a little, caught off guard. "Exactly like me, most people thought."

"Is she pretty?"

"You would want to know that."

"I only meant . . . "

"Alma's quite beautiful, yes. Of the two of us, much the better looking." Fayge shrugged. "I have a photograph, but it wouldn't be—it's from thirty-seven, thirty-eight."

"Will you show me, if we ever find where we are and come back from here?" Raissa grinned.

Fayge made a vague assenting sound. Then, "It's not in the apartment. It's here, on me. I'm not going to get it wet."

"Look, I know where we are! It's Jerozolim street, just, backward and from the other way . . . Oh, God, Fayge, why do they sit there, against the wall like that?"

"Raissa!" Fayge had never seen Beniek's sister without a rolling limp, but she ran now, without a thought for cover, or safety; heedless that there might be Arrow Cross or worse.

She ran towards the dead. They sat, and waited, and even from so many paces away in the rain Fayge knew there was no help for them. Against the bright-plastered wall of the greengrocer's on Jerozolim street, there were darker smears; and the smears led down to the people who sat on the pavement. Fayge winced, not for her ankle, and went after Raissa.

There were seven of them, all women, and they had not been shot. Raissa hesitated at the wrought-iron gate of the greengrocer's yard, and felt Fayge come panting behind her. She stammered, very softly, and one hand was fast around one bar of the gate.

"Raissa, come away. They're dead. Come away."

"Nobody shot them," Raissa whispered. "Look."

"I am looking." The eyes of seven women, flat and bright. Fayge broke her gaze from theirs.

Raissa kicked over something, some scrap on the pavement. "A permit," she said. "They had permits. Fayge, what—why bring them here, if they had permits, why bring them all the way here from Dzielna just to kill them? Why not shoot them, in front of all of us . . . with all of us?"

"Raissa, *come back*."

Fayge closed her eyes. The cry, when it came, was not like any sound she had ever heard. It was suffocated mercifully fast by the harsh one of a starved woman being sick.

"Butchers," came a gasp in broad Yiddish. "Butchers and monsters! Pregnant women!"

Before the noise could rise and bring murder down on them both, Fayge took three steps into the cobbled yard. She wrenched Raissa back by the collar. And she saw. All of them, clothing twisted aside, laid open below the ribs by the strange angled slash of a bayonet; more blood and water than seven lifetimes should see.

She turned aside, and retched bread and bile. *No,* she heard, inside her head. "No, no, no, I can't, no . . . "

"Fayge." Raissa's face was young and terrible. "They took . . . "

She would have folded with sickness, again, but the street-light popped and the light shifted, and she saw eyes that were pearl-pale gray. No bullet wound to mar the forehead; they would not have wasted one when death would come, besides, another way . . .

"It's Talia. Mendel's Talia."

"Yes."

Raissa had to turn her face against her jacket. "Ah, God. God."

"What do I tell Mendel?"

"I don't think we tell him." Raissa rubbed a soaked hand across her cold throat, to rid the hoarseness. She had to close her eyes, rather than look down again; and they burned. "When this is over," she said, shaking, "when this is over, no one will ever believe us. No one will believe these things could be."

"Raissa, you're sick . . . "

"So were you!"

"No, you're burning up, you're ill—"

Raissa waved Fayge's hand away. Her arms disappeared inside her jacket sleeves, and there was a moment's twist and struggle; without unbuttoning the jacket, Raissa dragged her shirt off by the collar. Fayge could glimpse her collarbones, bare and tidemarked with the night's grime, where the old tawny leather left them exposed. Raissa spread the shirt, white and dripping, over the red and darker red that should not have been laid bare.

Then she moved from Talia's body, backwards. Her boot caught a loose cobble and she would have gone down, on her back, into a puddle that was half blood. Fayge caught her under the elbows, too quick for anyone so weary, and too strong for anyone so small.

"Thank you," Fayge said, before Raissa could get it out.

[January 1942]

75

Everything was still. The key in the lock half woke her, so that in the darkness she put her hand down to the orange crate that was her daughter's cradle; then cold air rushed into the cold room and drove out the last of sleep. The moon was high, throwing its glitter against the frost-feathered window, when she opened her eyes.

"Fayge?"

She sat up, into brittle chill that made her teeth clench, and spared a hand from the eiderdown only long enough to push the hair from her face. "Beni," she managed.

But for his expression, she would have dived back into the pillows. He was paler than the winter night could make him, and deep-drawn lines hung under his eyes.

"I thought you would be gone," he whispered. "Singing . . ."

"Not tonight."

Beniek closed the door. Still in hat and gloves he crossed the room, two strides, and leaned his weight on his hands in the window's sill. "Go back to sleep, Fayge."

Wrapped in the quilt she rose. "Why did the Council keep you so late? What's wrong?"

"Nothing," he said. "Just talking." He turned and lifted her in his arms, because her feet were bare; her greeting kiss landed awry when he would not face her.

"Beniek —"

"What makes a man good, Fayge?"

"What?"

"How do you know if the things you do are good?"

"I don't know," she replied, into his shoulder.

"I mean it . . ."

"I'm sorry," she said. "What you're asking, I don't know how to answer."

He cleared his throat. "It's late. It's cold. I didn't mean to

76

wake you up." Beniek released her, to crouch beside Mir'ele's orange crate. Snow from his coat and trousers pooled on the floor. He took off his gloves and let them fall, and Fayge thought he would wake the child, by the harsh fall of his breath, by the chill in his fingertips on her small forehead; but he never touched her, his hand only drifting a moment, some centimeters from Mir'ele's hair.

On his feet again, and closer to Fayge than he had been for weeks, he filled all the cold space in the room. Beniek ran one hand through his hair, though it crackled and in the end looked worse. He was still, just breathing, close enough but not closing with her; he lowered his head, but not to look into her eyes.

"I didn't mean for it to be like this."

"Beni?"

"I married you to take you out of danger," he went on, perhaps explaining. "I didn't mean to bring you here."

Here was the Ghetto, here was everything that terrified her and made her forget she even had a name, here was a torn blouse and an armband crusted and stained. When she caught his gaze, she could see it, and she knew he knew.

"Beni," she said, "it's all right." That was what people said to each other.

"I loved you. Forgive me. I loved you."

He touched her then. He picked her up, suddenly so she had to throw her arms round his shoulders or unbalance, and the eiderdown fell and she was pressed against him in her shawl and her slip.

"Hello," Fayge said, half laughing, when he kissed her earnest and wild as a boy. The shawl came down from her shoulders and he pulled, pushed it the rest of the way. Bruises in the moonlight, tinting the places his hands had not yet been. A moment's silence as breath stopped, for both of them, as she tried to cast her hair forward and he brushed it away. Beniek's palm was still cold; it swept the curve of her shoulder, down to her breast, catching, possessive and painful. He cursed, words he had never used, words she had never heard, and threw her back so hard and sharply that plaster scraped through her slip.

Caught between him and the wall she cried out, as his buttons scored down her skin and his free hand went around the back of her neck, and he lifted her without tenderness or invitation. His mouth was hot and smeary in her hair, and the only space for her to breathe was the hollow between his throat and shoulder, so that the scent of sweat and of him was all she knew for a moment. He was still familiar, in her, around her, after so long; he was her husband, or something like him.

"Beniek," she tried, whisper rising to a wail as he bit beneath her ear. "Benyamin, you're hurting—"

"Whore."

He was crying before she wrested a hand free, before she hit him across the cheek. A torrent of salt between their bodies, and falling from his eyes into hers; Beniek let go of her, her legs went nerveless and he did not try to keep her from the floor.

"Fayge."

Her eyes were closed, and she had crooked one knee against the ache in her belly.

"Fayge." He knelt and covered her left hand with his. If she moved, it was not meant.

"Fayge, I'm sorry, please." He picked her up, as easily as he ever had, and there was featherbed instead of floor, and the eiderdown streaked over with dust and damp. Warmth came back into her skin, though it could not reach her bones; he stood over her, still, without speaking again.

When he stooped to kiss her forehead she reached up, quick as his blood, and drew him down to her mouth. So he could taste the damage there, find the path of his own teeth, know that hate tasted coppery even in this cold.

*

"So, speak to me of next week," Beniek said, as he cut a two-kilo loaf in fifteen parts. "They want something serious. No musicals."

"Good, we can eat the musicians!"

"Oh shut up, skirt-diver," Mendel called out. Raissa leaned back in the one chair, a little startled, before she grinned. The winter, and the long sickening hunger, had made them all bitter as wine and fearless as wolves.

"Shut up," Beniek agreed. He tossed the cut bread forward, and who caught a piece caught it, and it was their share; almost fair. "Raissa, what have we got?"

"Something in translation . . . frogs? Euripides, I think. It was Violeta's. And *The Dybbuk*, but there's not enough parts in *The Dybbuk*. Might try some Teyve the Milkman, but that's no good without songs—"

"Wonderful. Greek frogs or grave spirits."

"Better go with *The Dybbuk*, I think," Hirsh said.

"But everyone's seen *The Dybbuk* before."

He shook his head, finishing a mouthful. "Euripides, it's not what we're about. We have good enough sources in the Yiddish. We have Ansky; we don't need classical shit."

"I think the classics appropriate, since we have all made the choice of Achilles."

The silence was long.

"Dear God, Fayge just made an allusion." Raissa laughed, a half-tone false.

"Fayge has an education," she said, colder than the room. "A Western education, with no Jew-quotas, and no religious tripe. And *The Frogs* is Aristophanes."

"We couldn't help the quotas!"

"Provincials," said Fayge, and went back to her script.

"Yes, well, you liked my provincial brother well enough."

"He liked me. Or at least, he was very eager. Why don't you ask him?"

Sheyndl gaped, squeaking when her needle veered from her thimble and into her finger. Raissa turned, temper warming, to see what Beniek would say, but he seemed not to have heard. The quiet settled again, and the jaw-aching cold.

"Good morning, Jews! *Hande hoch!*"

The great doors groaned open, sending snow amidst the empty seats. Down the center aisle strode Hans Murer, with his cloak billowing behind. Black cloak, and black leather raincoat beneath it; demon's wings. Raissa followed orders and put her hands above her head and wondered if he had come direct from his Hell.

"How nice to find all of you together. Damn, but it's cold in here." He went to the piano, flung back the lid, and picked out a jaunty *Maple Leaf Rag*, slightly off tempo, more like a march . . .

Lithuanians, Arrow Cross, were coming up the aisle. Ten of them—enough to secure the whole theatre, never mind half a troupe of half-starved people—in fur-topped boots, fur-lined coats and round fur hats. Their rifles were at ease across their backs, but when Murer stopped playing, the guns clicked and cracked to the ready.

"Jews, it's very simple. You don't even have to line up, because I've got to see to so many more of you. Consider it an especial favor, I came down to visit you myself." He closed the piano, and went on. "All you have to do is figure out if you're at the front of the alphabet or the back."

Raissa's arms were shivering with pain. She slackened them a little, and Murer pounced.

"Don't tell me you need help. Now, if we can go on? If your surname starts with A, B, and so on through G, you're going for a little stroll with these merry officers. I told you it was simple. I'd bring a coat."

He turned, gave the Party salute to the Arrow Cross men, and jumped down from the stage. When he had gone everyone's arms came down, slowly; there was no need to collect coats and scarves, because everyone wore everything they owned. Only Raissa, who wrote with rolled-up sleeves, had to stoop for her jacket and Passiert.

"Damn, I'm still Gellerman," she said, mildly, shouldering into the jacket. Hirsh's arm slipped through hers, and she jumped.

"No, Hirsh."

"Someone's got to haul you through the snow."

"If this is my death, I'll face it standing straight up," she said. "No, Hirsh."

"Don't flatter yourself. I'm still Glik," he echoed her.

"Let's hope so." She had given up punning his name in grammar school, but the rifles were near and shining.

Seven of them, from fifteen, filed out onto the hard snow: Mendel Avram, Sheyndl Berkowitz, Gellermans, Glik. Raissa tried to imagine the roll of the Great Synagogue, tried to count how many people the surname-selection meant. She had gotten through ten surnames with seven, eight people each, keeping tally with the flotsam in her pockets, before they reached the Umschlagplatz.

There were no trains, yet. Just the entire Jewish Police, arrayed in a cordon in the cold sunshine; there must have been some borrowed from Siauliai, too, from Kovno. At the top of the cordon, on the pavement near the tracks, a platform had been built, broad enough for two guards and a chair; there was a man in the chair, and he was not a German.

"It's Gens. I think we should bow."

"Or spit." Raissa stamped, to knock the snow out of her boots. A gust flapped the edge of Fayge's ridiculous coat, sending it out like a sail, and Hirsh and Raissa both turned. In such cold, she kept it buttoned fast around her daughter.

"Give her to me," Beniek was saying, low, but never expecting defiance.

"No!"

"Fayge, they won't take her from me."

"At least one would die, if they took her from me."

"You're both wrong, give her to me."

Hirsh and Fayge shouted at the same time, but Raissa scooped Mir'ele into her arms.

"Hello, oytzer. You got as big as me while I wasn't looking. And my God, you can scream when it pleases you!"

"Raissa, give me my child or I will murder you where you stand."

"Why not wait a minute and let them do it? Save you a sweat." She shook her head, and went on over the soaring of Mir'ele's shrieks. "This many of them, Fayge, it means killing. Think of yourself." She hefted the toddler onto her hip, rummaged her vest pocket and came up with a quarter-ration's bread. "Cork it, little one."

"Raissa!"

"Come on, Hirsh, don't you scream too, I'm out of bread." Raissa shot him a smile, flicked her Passiert wallet, and stepped into the cordon, to face the baton and Gens.

He was calm, pale and the image of dignity, in his fine Hussar's coat, until she reached him. She breathed in hard, held it, and held out her papers, but he never looked at them. The small neat man went into a white-edged rage, and knocked her proffered hand aside.

"You stupid girl! Where's your husband? Come through

the line together, how fucking stupid can you be?"

Raissa stared. Her papers could not declare her more husbandless. Maybe the poor man had lost his mind, in the face of so many people, waiting on his word . . . She could not make her teeth meet to clench round the fear, so her mouth was hanging open, she knew. Arrow Cross boys were poised at her left and right, the guards at the underworld's gates; they were expressionless, and so young, with Schmeissers in their arms and the ceremonial quivers on their backs, fletching all blue and silver caught by the sun, as if this was a parade and not a murder.

"Move it, you idiots, send her husband through!"

She turned. They had seized Hirsh and pulled him into the cordon, and he was faint with fear, bewildered, and they cuffed him and kicked him and shouted. "Hey, bastard, you forgot your kid and your wife!"

"Raissa, what—"

She put her hand up to blot some blood from his forehead, but never touched him: the Arrow Crossman nearest swung her by the elbow, and tossed Hirsh after her.

To the right.

"The right," Hirsh muttered, astonished. A limping girl, a skinny shop foreman, and a three-year-old child, and they stood where there was life. Raissa handed Mir'ele to him and swayed to the cobblestones, toppled by relief. She sat there a while, her head down on her knees, until he nudged her with his foot.

"*Pass'auf*," he hissed to her, "Pay attention. It's their turn. Look."

Beniek walked so like a king, she thought, though the men with their guns trained on him, in the brown ill-cut uniform of the Jewish Police, had been his playmates as a child. His steps were slow, measured to Fayge's smaller stride, and curses could not make him hurry.

They were not plain curses, and Raissa could see Fayge's eyes narrow as the Yiddish went beyond her and she fought to understand. It was Raissa's own tongue, and she needed no such help, though she wished for ignorance, wished she had never been given ears.

"Go on, Jew-killer, list-maker."

"You first, old man, straight on the trains, you before my sons, *you fucking first* . . . ."

"Hurry up, *schreyber,* it's a long walk to Ponar!"

Writer confused Fayge, maybe; *Ponar* did not. Just at Gens' feet she whirled, to bolt, to break free, and for it she got a rifle-butt between the shoulders. The first man of the Ghetto only prodded her with his baton when she slumped, and started berating Beniek. "You're all morons! Where's the child? Man, woman, child! A German could understand it! Go back for your kid, you jackass, move!"

He froze. Raissa saw her brother unmoving, saw the boy in blue and silver lean from the left.

Fayge picked herself up, and ran back down the cordon's length. Far back in the crowd there came a wail, clear and high, and it struck through the silent, the starving, the resigned and dispirited. It was *no!* even if it was wordless. The lines of policemen did not move when the crowd surged, except at the very front, beyond Raissa's sight, where they seemed to heft something along like a sack.

Someone had put a vicious scratch down Fayge's cheek, and her golden hair was all unpinned. She had both arms braced around a boy about six years old. Raissa recognized him for the youngest of the innumerable Berkowitzes, but surely Fayge had never seen him in her life.

"My God," Hirsh said, as the three were waved to the right. "My God, it's a show."

They stood in the cold for four hours, long after Raissa had stopped feeling her hands beneath her vest. The gold-topped baton flashed left or right, right or left, and over everything that hoarse eagle-voice was shouting, "Man! Woman! Child!"

[February 1942]

The snow had stopped. It was too cold for snow. On the stage a small and smoky brazier, with the evening potatoes in its embers, gave warmth enough for pages to be turned without gloves. There were six potatoes among eighteen people, and the orchestra demanded a double share; so no one now had spoken for half an hour. Raissa, with her hands inside her shirt and her head bowed against the slow strange dizziness of hunger, stared at the same ten lines of dialogue and waited for someone to lash out. They were not so hungry, yet, that there could be no rehearsal; but Beniek was not there. It was half past six, and the director had not come.

"Fayge," she hissed, risking everyone's temper.

From sleep, it seemed, Fayge lifted her head; her hair was fallen loose across her eyes, and the uppermost page of her script was upside-down.

"Fayge, where is he?"

Fayge kept silent, because it was not worth speaking or wondering into the bitter air; but her brows were drawn in uncertainty, or fear. Raissa edged her pocket watch across the boards, sparing just enough movement to put it in Fayge's clear view; she saw the younger woman's expression flicker, through the hunger-haze, in alarm.

"The Herr Direktor called us for four-thirty," Sheyndl ventured, though it was muffled by the vast cold all around. "It's gone past, hasn't it?"

"Long past, while we starve!" It was Mendel, the pianist, who spoke; and his fingers were blue and his eyes were red.

"Take my share then, and choke on it!"

Raissa put her head in her hands, to blind herself to the fight, but Fayge did not speak again. There was a soft flurry of movement, of paper and scarf and a long worn coat, more than any of them had energy to expend; Fayge had gone to the pit's edge, and jumped off.

"Brought you a candle . . . "

"I can't read Yiddish," Fayge replied. "So it's just as well in the dark."

"I can put it in German then, won't take a minute."

"You can write German!"

"Yes," said Raissa, and kept back the *of course*. She tilted a music stand and fixed the candle there, in an uneasy bed of wax.

"Why have I spent six months staring at these chicken tracks?"

"You never said anything before." Raissa shrugged and turned the blank side of a page, and started copying dialogue in round lazy Roman hand. "Mendel doesn't mean it, you know. Everyone's so hungry "

"Not hungry. Starving," said Fayge in Yiddish. "We're starving."

"All right, we are." Raissa paused. "But they must feed you, surely, the Germans . . . "

Fayge, fierce, laughed. "Thirty deca of bread and three grams of margarine, same as they feed you!"

From above there was the ringing sound of metal in the cold. Fayge stood, and remembered to offer a hand to Raissa; they waited, for one person with rag-wrapped steps or many with fur-lined boots against the cold. Neither sound came.

"Frau Gellerman! Frau Gellerman! In God's name quick, Frau Gellerman!"

It was Leyb, in the blue and white shirt of the Judenrat couriers, and he was barefoot.

"Come," he gasped out, as soon as he saw them. His cap

tumbled backward off his head but he was running, heedless, back the way he came.

Darkness and snow and the painful gleam of streetlights on the icy pavement, with a cold so sharp Fayge buckled for a moment. Raissa had left her jacket behind.

A sound ripped the night across, sharp and held long and clear by the cold. It came to Fayge like a scream and Raissa heard a roar, but when they ran, into the dark, they kept pace with each other.

The street was empty; all the windows were terribly dark. The Judenrat alone was lit, warm, blinding; on every floor in every pane was the part-unfamiliar yellow glow of electric light. There was a car at the curb; Fayge flung up an arm to catch Raissa.

"Oh, fucking God in hell."

" . . . Fayge?"

Fayge bent, for a moment, nearly into a snowbank. "He's here."

Raissa meant to ask, and only wheezed.

"Kittel's here," Fayge repeated, a name Raissa had never heard; she could read it, for a moment, on the steam in the deathly-chill air. Fayge was gone, half sliding downhill, and at the doors of the Judenrat dogs were shrilling, men were shouting.

There were dead men on the snow.

"Herr Gutgestalt, please, tell me—my husband—" Fayge's voice was young and pathetic and in the dark, so sharply shadowed, Raissa could see neither truth nor artifice.

"Have they taken him away from here? Herr Gutgestalt, please!" She was past him then, by pity or force, a slender darkness moving fast. She had remembered to grab Raissa's elbow.

"What did he tell you? Where's Beni? Where's my brother?"

It was dizzying hot, and crowded, on the lower floor of the building. There was jostling and swearing and breathtaking shoves in the back, and the two of them seemed to be moving in precisely the wrong direction. Jewish Police and Arrow Cross militia choked the stairwell, and it seemed they would be crushed or tumbled backward.

Shots howled off the walls then, and the stairs emptied, but Fayge rushed on. Corridors, offices, Raissa stumbled through them at Fayge's pace, cold in the knowledge that they moved toward danger.

One of the office doors had had the glass knocked from its frame; from inside, there was the bitter burning smell of cordite. The room was full, desks and rolling chairs all aside: there were two Arrow Cross, two dogs and an SS officer—the blue-eyed one—Kittel, and a gun.

Beniek lay haloed in darkening blood. His eyes were open, and in one hand and scattered all around him, plain white paper: every page blank. Fayge ducked between the dogs' forepaws and fell, sparrow-small and silent, and Raissa followed in the shocked path she made.

Raissa cleared away the cheap blank paper, to find his hand, and to find that it was not cold. Fayge reached, flinched, and cradled her husband's head in her hands, a mess underneath of gray and red-flecked white.

"Don't touch. Don't touch." Raissa was warning her, or babbling, but Fayge bent forward, until her forehead touched his, until her blonde hair was heavy and dark with his blood.

"Get up!" Kittel snapped. He was not the same kind of monster, in his build, that Murer was; he was only a head taller than Raissa, and wiry. But when he spoke, the dogs strained and snarled, and Raissa leapt out of the way. "Breyderl," she muttered, once and again, for Beniek; but she did not want to die with him.

"*Aufstehen!*"

Fayge did not stir. One of her palms pressed against the sticky floor, but it was only to brace for what came next. The truncheon was not a hollow one, and there was glass along its length, because it belonged to Kittel. It caught her across the shoulders, and Raissa crammed her fingers into her mouth and backed half over the desk and did not scream.

"Get up, you stupid girl, my dinner's waiting!"

Maybe she had fainted; Kittel himself grabbed her by elbow and coat-collar, and lifted her, and heaved.

"Take them out of here, and nail his head to the Strashun gate —what's left of his head. Put up a nice sign about listmakers who don't make lists." He paused, to wipe his gun on his jacket. "And get a bloody cleaning detail out here. What a mess."

[February 1942]

HOW THE RIVER SCREAMS

"Your picture in my hand, your name burning on my tongue: mine whom I abandoned, regent of my night."
—S. Taaffe

She sat on the floor with her back against the wall in the communal dressing room, closed her eyes and wished herself somewhere silent. The baby was heavy against her breast, small legs thumping the vague rhythms of sleep on her ribs, and Beniek was nowhere to be found, yet, to carry the child home.

"Fayge! Fayge, the Germans have business with you." Beniek's sister, who spoke passable German and had a flair for a dramatic entrance, came careening in the dressing-room doorway. By unspoken command everyone got out of her way, and the noise in the room rustled down to a miserable quiet. If the Germans had reason to stay past the final curtain, better not to be heard.

"The Germans? Who?" Fayge got up, without handing Mir'ele to anybody. The toddler stirred and murmured and stayed asleep.

"I don't know. Three of them, and the Commandant."

"Oberscharführer," Fayge corrected, knowing she would be ignored.

"They're out front, and if you don't go, Fayge, they've lined people up to shoot."

"How many?"

Raissa stared at her. "Ten."

Fayge shifted Mir'ele onto her hip, waking her this time, and followed Raissa.

There were four uniforms, four pairs of shining knee-boots and four guns, but only one officer did the talking, and Fayge half knew before he opened his mouth what he would say.

"Fraulein—"

"It's Frau," she risked, "Frau Gellerman."

"Yes, of course," he said, all courtesy. "I recall seeing you on the Vienna stage."

She waited.

"The officers' canteen here is in need of a singer. We wished to extend this opportunity to you."

"Thank you, Herr Oberscharführer, I will consider—"

"We are in, you understand, we are in need of an immediate answer." He reached forward then, and his black-gloved hand curled in a caress over Mir'ele's hair. "Such a position would guarantee the necessary permits for your child as well as yourself."

She froze, and saw nothing but that dark blur on her daughter's bright hair. Raissa kicked her in the heel, and everyone was looking at her, but his hand was on Mir'ele's head and she could not look away. She tightened her hold until Mir'ele struggled and screamed.

"Are you listening, Frau Gellerman?"

"I'll take it. Thank you. Yes, I'll sing. I'll take it."

*

Raissa was awake when the knock came. She sat up, stretched and took off her glasses to rub the bridge of her nose; there was no chance of her getting up before the door swung open, anyway.

Beniek's wife stood in the doorway, bleeding from the mouth, holding her shoes in one hand. She looked from Violeta's sleeping form on the studio couch, to Raissa behind her typewriter; she said nothing, and Raissa got onto her feet, still holding a sheet of paper.

"Are you—my God, hold still, I'll wake Violeta."

"Violeta's awake," she said, sleepily, rising to shadow Raissa's candlelight.

"So, I guess you sang for them?"

Fayge grimaced. "I'm sorry for knocking here so late. I can't, I couldn't go home like this . . . "

"It's no trouble," said Violeta.

"I was awake," chimed Raissa. Her coffee-colored eyes were overbright from tiredness, and her voice was raspy in Fayge's ringing ears. She sat down again, because that was the only way all three people fit into the room with the door shut. "See? Writing." She gestured to the desk, and scattered pages under the wide couch and onto the floor.

Fayge bent for one of them. "Chava, the heroine, a beautiful girl . . . ?" She found Raissa's eraser and rubbed the words out. "Not if it's going to be me, playing Chava. I hardly have a face left, I think."

"You'll be all right," Violeta disagreed. "It won't swell more than it has."

"I just need to get cleaned up. He can't see me like this. He won't understand. I can't make him understand."

"What would be worse, you taking our couch until that stops bleeding, or him seeing you and getting it over with?" Violeta slid, sideways, to the water bucket and dipped her handkerchief. "Be serious. Tell me. I should be awake, anyway, we've got till tomorrow to finish this play and my beloved has no work ethic."

"My beloved was asleep," Raissa shot back. "It's no good, Vi, her staying here."

"It's gone three o'clock," said Violeta. "It's no good her doing anything else." She sat on the desk in order to stand again on the other side of it, leaving Fayge's path clear to the curtained-off studio couch. And Fayge meant to say no, or something like it, because Beniek would talk; but the last thing she remembered was the narrow slice of light that came through the wavering blanket curtain, and the low back-and-forth richness of their voices amid the clack, clack of Raissa's typewriter.

[October 1941]

"Faygelein."

"Sir?" She had started to slip from beneath the covers; he caught her at the wrist, and pulled her back to him.

"Listen. You can't go back tonight. Stay here. It's safer."

"I can't," she echoed him.

"We've got to make room in that pit of a Ghetto for eight thousand more, and it's happening tonight. I want you here." He kissed the knuckles of the hand he held.

"My daughter is there."

A sharp-drawn breath, but not yet of rage. "I forgot," he admitted. "I forgot there was a child. How old?"

"Two years."

"Is she on your papers, or your bloody husband's?" He shook his head. "No matter. It's still too young."

Fayge gazed into the blind white of the pillow, rather than meet his eyes, the same shade as hers and colder. He spoke again. He chose his words with care; he always did. It made him dangerous.

"I know some people who'll hide a Jewish kid. The little convent, you know, not the cathedral, the one over the river?"

"Sir, with respect—"

"I said I knew a place," he repeated, "I didn't say Murer knew. And if Murer doesn't know, Hingst doesn't know. So only I know, and I really don't see better odds for you than that."

"You could have her killed!"

"Yes." He shrugged. "But then you wouldn't sing for me." A hand on her breast. "It costs money. I don't know how much you have, but it's not cheap."

Fayge left the bed, and stood in the firelight to gather her clothes, unspeaking. He watched her dress, as he always did.

"Think about it, Faygelein."

*

"Raissa, I need to borrow some money."

Raissa folded her book around her fingers. She did not goggle, but it was a near thing. "What, Beniek's run out?"

"Beni doesn't need to come into this."

"I've got fifty zloty, something like that, twenty rubles—"

"I need it in marks," Fayge interrupted.

"You need to get an idea, then. Beniek's got my half of what Father left."

"But you know where he keeps it!"

"Of course I know; they're my rubles." Raissa tipped in her chair, until the wild ends of her hair brushed the studio couch. "How much?"

"Some thousands," Fayge said, her voice fading miserably. "I know it's—I wouldn't have come to see you if—"

"What will you give me?"

"Anything I have!"

Raissa shook her head, one quick decisive shake, so that Fayge's eyes darkened damp with the failure; in the strange light from the greased-paper window, it seemed she lost several inches of height.

"Is it important?" Maybe the cough was roughening Raissa's voice. "No, don't tell me, I don't want to know. If you can't tell my brother, you'd better not tell me."

"It's important. It's my life."

The front legs of Raissa's chair thumped. "Go home."

"Please—"

"Go home, and take out the third brick from the left of the third joint of stovepipe. You'll have to stand on a chair, I should think. Clean up the little plaster bits or he'll know. There's seven hundred thousand—cash—belongs to me."

"Seven hundred thousand," Fayge repeated, a little wildly.

"Don't bother leaving a receipt."

*

Fayge rubbed thumb and forefinger nervously across the wallet that held her *Passiert,* not a false one, and five thousand marks, as real. If it was as easy as everyone said, then leaving the Ghetto by the gate was only a matter of timing. Timing and money. She wore a raincoat to the ankles, a muffler and a hat, but she felt naked. Her fair hair was cast over her face by the wind. The rucksack she carried was heavy, and she gave it one last heave by the straps before pressing her hands down in the raincoat's pockets and keeping them there.

Breathing was harder than walking. Under the last arched bridge before the picket-and-wire she went dizzy, and nearly collapsed, her cheek coming hard against black brick lichen-damp. She wiped her face, scrupulously, with cold fingers. She found a compact mirror in one of her pockets and made her expression very still.

It was heavy, what she carried, and she was not used to

bearing the weight behind her shoulder blades. Sweating, and chilly, shaking, and hot, Fayge swallowed and took a few more steps. There was nothing now, under the sky white with cold cloud, to hide her from the men at the gate. Burdened, and moving so, fawn-timid in shoes with no heels, she thought she must look about twelve years old.

It was taller than she had known, the Strashun gate, three times Beniek's height and broad as the avenue. There were Arrow Cross police, in plain service brown, standing armed on both sides.

There was one man in black picked out with red and silver, and he paced in front of the gate with his hands clasped in the small of his back, contemplatively smoking a rank cigarette. He was waiting for something to happen on the Aryan side of the gate, and around the cigarette he was smiling. Fayge pulled herself into an alley-shadow, not leaning back against anything, and waited with him.

The Arrow Cross had dogs, but they were choked and wore dull steel muzzles; she knew about the dogs. She tried to tell the hour by the sun, but there was no sun, and she had never learned how.

There was a scrabble and a scraping from somewhere above her, and something skinny and coal colored dropped to the pavement.

"Frau *Gellerman*?"

"Leyb!" It was the boy from the theatre, the boy whose twin, she couldn't remember what had happened to the twin, the girl. The only clean part of him was his eyes, and a bow of sacking around his middle was spilling what looked like cabbage leaves.

"I didn't know you went—out." From under whatever rag covered his torso, he dragged an immaculately white shirt, and stuck his arms into the sleeves. It bore the bright blue and yellow six-point star of the Judenrat, and it was his *carte blanche*. Leyb buttoned it over cabbages and all.

"Frau Gellerman, you can't go by the gate, not today. There's trucks on the road, you know, lorries, coming here. *Seleckja* soon, you know. Trucks? You can't go on the road."

"I have to get out," she said, gently, in the best Yiddish she could manage to match his chewed-husk German.

"No, no way. Tonight, *Seleckja*! I'm, for the Judenrat, I'm a runner boy, I know!"

"I know, too."

"So you can't go. That man? At the gate? Murer. He'll kill you, and if he don't kill you, you'll go on the trucks."

"I have to get out."

Leyb cocked his head on one side, and darted past her, around her, to get at her rucksack's flap. He tugged on it, though she threw her weight away from him, and he whistled.

"Guess you'd better not go out the gate, all right."

"But I—"

"You go under," he told her, and took one of her hands and pulled. "If you're small enough. I'll show the place. Frau Gellerman, your husband, he'll have the skin off my ass for his hat!"

Fayge smiled, though her heart had tumbled and flipped.

"You look like them," Leyb observed, trotting. "You'll be all right. But it's really stupid, to leave by the gate. Don't you know they stick your bag with bayonets?"

She was breathing, surely, but there was no air.

"Frau Gellerman! Whoa! Frau Gellerman!"

[February 1942]

Raissa had coughed all night. No other sound found its way into Fayge's dreams: though the Russians were shelling the riverbank, hard, the long guns were not what she heard.

Fayge got out of bed. The nights were still cold enough, now, for the stove to be lit, but there was no coal. Even the Germans had no coal. She put on her shawl and knelt, in the dark, to rummage her coat. It took her a moment, fingers sorting carefully over schnapps flasks and stockings, razors and stray lentils, to find the bottle she wanted. It was dark heavy glass, and only so big as her hand. It meant two weeks' bread for the entire theatre, and it was for selling.

She parted the curtain and moved into Raissa's candle-light.

There was a notebook in her hand and a pen tucked under her thumb, but she lay gasping, with her head tipped back, and the ink had long dried on the nib. Her eyes were dulled with pain. The rag she held to her lips was soaked through, to the very corners, and her pillows were spattered dark in the half-darkness, bloody.

"Ah, God."

"Fayge?"

"Here." Fayge handed over the bottle. Raissa hitched her weight onto one elbow, and tried the stopper. Sharp, the sudden scent of alcohol and herbs.

"Cough syrup," Raissa said, and grinned.

"Codeine," Fayge corrected.

"My God, it's not for me, then!" Cheerily, though her voice was a thread, she handed the bottle back.

"It is."

"I can't pay you for this."

In the wild, dim light Raissa thought Fayge looked hurt. "Why can no one just take something from me? Why do you all bring up payment?"

"Because the ones that hate you think you can be paid for anything, and the ones who love you know what it costs you to get it." Raissa paused. "Thanks."

Fayge shrugged. She turned Raissa's pillows, clean side uppermost, and sat on the edge of the couch and toyed with the threadbare corner of Raissa's coverlet.

"Waiting to see if it kills me, then?"

"Yes. I'm not sure the German on the label matches with whatever it was in the Polish pharmacy they stole it from. It could be strychnine."

"Tasted like cough syrup." Raissa tried to laugh, and fell back.

"Damn."

Fayge smoothed Raissa's hair out of her eyes, because it was sticking damp with sweat or blood. Her hand stayed.

"Fayge?"

"Your hair is too long," she said, vaguely. "Go to sleep."

When Raissa tried to talk again, tried to ask Fayge . . . tried to ask her anything, there were no words she could remember. And Fayge was singing, in Yiddish, a very old song, *lovely as the moon, shining like the stars.* Fayge was singing.

[April 1943]

Leyb dug a knee into Fayge's back, slipped his fingers between brick and barbed wire, and put eyes and nose over the wall.

"No good," he said after a moment. "We're stuck!"

"What do you mean, no good?"

"I'm telling you, it's Kittel down there!"

"And I'm telling you it's not. I know what he looks like." She risked an inch more height, swaying under the combined weight of Leyb and ten kilos of lentils. "It's only Murer. We'll be all right."

"But the dogs, Fayge!"

"Fine, you want to do this after dark, then?"

"N-no."

He slid from her shoulders, his bare feet squelching into a puddle. Ice spiked its edges. The sun was low and sickly orange, bruise blue pressing down at the gates and arches and robbing the surety of their sight. With nightfall the gate guard would be doubled, and the Germans' moonlight, great stark ditch-lanterns, was no gift. Leyb stuck his tongue between his teeth, peered through a gap in the mortar, and shifted his load of potatoes.

"Over or under?" he asked, after a moment's eye for the dogs.

"No good going under, not here, we'd need ten clear minutes."

"Five," he argued.

"Five for you. You're the size of a minnow—maybe just the bones." Fayge straightened and shook off the fog that was half sleeplessness, half hunger; she offered her hand and shoulder to Leyb, braced herself to the wall and pitched him over.

She landed badly, herself, with a splash and a dull cry; the wire had ripped wool and skin at her wrist. She spared the injury long enough to see it was not pumping blood, then righted herself and turned down the alley after Leyb.

He was still in the avenue, and he was standing still.

"Fuh," Leyb gabbled. "F-Fayge!" He grabbed for her wrist, the hurt one, so that she cursed and shook him off; it made her turn, and look where he was looking.

In the gloom of the nearest arch there was the glint of a taut steel chain. The chain disappeared into the moon-pale ruff of a dog, and the dog had a red mouth flecked over with foam, and eyes that glittered hard as ruby, and someone held the chain and never spoke.

"Run," she whispered, shoving him hard behind her. "Now."

There was a single cold *clink*, and the chain fell down from the light. The dog surged, and growled, and was free.

*

They had managed to get the old gas-jets burning in the foot-lights, so that for this rehearsal, the stage was bright. The sets were freshly repainted, and the damp sour odor of bad lime-thinned paint was somewhat brought out by the heat; but Chelm stood, even if it was all cardboard, and Chelm had daylight. Easier, that way, to go on singing past the hour where supper should have fallen.

Something hit the fire door with a clang like a lead weight, blundered through the scrim, smeared the skim-milk-blue of the sky beyond Chelm.

"Save me," Fayge choked, "hide me!"

"Fayg'l!"

She was bleeding from somewhere, tears streamed into her nose and mouth, and with Raissa and Sheyndl and the chorus watching, she threw herself forward and felt for the stage beneath her hands and shivered and sobbed for air.

"Her coat," barked Raissa, to stop the staring. "Take the coat."

Mendel pulled her free of it, cursing at the weight; he struggled and half-carried, half-kicked it into the dark of the wings. Sheyndl scrambled after the water bucket, without being told; but Raissa, creaking and wincing, crouched at Fayge's side and hissed questions into her ear. She found a clean end of handkerchief and mopped Fayge's near cheek-bone with it, and waited for an answer.

"Behind me," Fayge said at last, still ragged and wheezing.

"How far? How long?"

"Lost him. Th' last turning."

"Stand up. You have to stand up, because you have to help *me* up. Wash your face, and get a script, and get on with it."

"He's coming," Fayge insisted, warning, wild, her blue eyes dazed and strange.

Raissa half staggered, half pushed the two of them upright. "You lost him. You said it yourself. You run fast. I've seen you."

"Your grammar is terrible," said Fayge at last. "Where did you learn German, from earthworms and chickens?"

"Just about."

Fayge passed a hand over her eyes, and shrugged her torn cardigan close, but let go of Raissa and moved without a falter. "Tell—tell me the cue, Mendl. Just tell me where to sing."

"Rais'le," Sheyndl mouthed into Raissa's hair, cupping one hand childish around the secret. "Him who?"

"No idea."

"I don't like it. Ha'n't ever seen her afraid!"

"You'd be afraid," Raissa answered, "if you'd ran for your life."

Everyone breathed normally again, after three or so minutes, and Fayge's arms stopped shivering, though she kept her bloodied hand tucked to her chest. It was four or so minutes, Raissa thought, before the back door opened again, and there was a gust of cold that did not subside.

One of the gas-jets popped and smoked and went dark. Fayge fell back, into the shadow it made, but all around her were quiet, and nervelessly still.

The cunningly painted town hall of Chelm rocked on its foundations, which were not real; it pitched and fell flat. A man stood where it had been, outlined in the gleam of sleet on his cloak, which was black and mud stained and terribly torn down the front. He was all black, a spectre, a demon of shadow with silver bolts at his throat; or he was a pale man, not even very tall, and the blackness of him was only his eyes, which were blue.

In his gloved hands, the only part of him not muffled in the cloak, he held an automatic pistol and a blood-daubed white handkerchief.

"Stand very still, Jews," he said, and they did. He let the safety off the gun, for all of them to see.

"Who can run? Who ran from me? Tell me, and some of you might live to run again."

No one answered. No one moved. Sheyndl whimpered, a little, and caught it, when Raissa trod on her foot.

"My name is Kittel. Do you know me, Jews? I've come from Siauliai. I've finished in Siauliai. Now all of you belong to me. Understand? Say yes." He dropped, then, the folds of his black cloak flapping up like wings; he swiped the handkerchief over the stage and brought it up smeared and bloody and wet.

Kittel began walking, then, with slow perfect paces, from man to woman and back again, circling; the red-white cloth like evidence in God's own court, like a brand. He turned his back, and gazed up at the painted sun in the painted pale sky. He whistled. "One of you ran me a race, a very good race, but it ends now."

He turned, and went for Fayge faster than had the dog.

"You, I think."

Her hand, untended, bled down the blue of her cardigan. He set the pistol against her forehead and canted his head on one side, considering.

Fayge closed her eyes.

Kittel grabbed her injured hand with his free one, so fast Raissa thought the gun would go off. For a second it seemed he examined the cut, appraising it, deep and clean. Then, blood and all, he kissed Fayge's palm.

"Not today," said Kittel, and put the gun beneath his cloak.

[June 1943]

III.

It was the second cigarette they had smoked in their entire lives, and Mikah nicked it from Rina's case on her dresser. He handed it to Hirsh, leaned on the balcony railing, and watched the war. Below them, the swastika on its blood-colored ground unfurled along Strashun. Soldiers, following, shook the pavements, and their crisp columns seemed to stretch for miles. He could see them out on the river bridge, ants along a twig.

Hirsh coughed, flicking away the cigarette. There was ash on the lapel of his narrow black coat, and he took the coat off rather than brush the ash away, because there would be no getting to the yeshiva.

The morning had not started out any differently. Hirsh davened, and Mikah did the breakfast washing-up in his shirtsleeves. He had left the Ramayles Yeshiva the year before, without telling their parents why.

His brother's thoughts on God were not something either of them needed to speak about. Hirsh had God, really had him, the way Mikah had his violin, and that was all. They had never had this twin-language Rina talked about, just maybe a kind of twinned thought, always silent. Mikah could fill up the gaps in his brother's long holy quiet, and Hirsh could have told anyone what the violin was saying.

Rina, three years older, was a nurse at the Levite hospital downtown. Every morning she flew around the apartment like a wild bird trapped, hunting up her bag and her starched white hat, and moving too fast to avoid half the furniture. Berek, her fiancé, managed to still be sleeping, and in the large bedroom off the kitchen, Mikah could hear his father beginning his prayers. He stood the last teacup in the drainer and Rina took it, clattering all the cutlery, to pour herself a cup to bring with her out the door. The clock wheezed and chimed for seven, though it was really a quarter past, and Mikah dried his hands on his vest and took down his violin.

It was an aged instrument, strung with stories of press gangs and Cossacks, pegs mellowed not with rosin-dust but years. It was tuned to the sons of genteel exiled poverty, to the wailing winter nights of the Pale, and to Mikah. He was the oldest son, if you wanted to come down to it, and Hirsh had never shown love or aptitude for playing. He could play, a little, because Mikah had shown him, but it was Mikah's fiddle.

Because the sound of the tuning fork went into Hirsh's teeth and upset his prayers, today Mikah played without tuning. About six bars of Borodin, and then on, away, in flight: the kind of music that belonged to him and never got set on paper. He played for Hirsh's morning rites, something like a nigun; then of a sudden his fingers stopped moving at all, and under the bow the strings cried out.

Hirsh leaped up, to stare where Mikah stared.

Mikah stilled the strings with his fingertips, set the violin back in its case, and threw back the balcony curtains, and then the doors.

Outside, the cavalry was just passing, slow and stately as

they could do and still fight the hill. In the horsemen's wake the river breeze carried up the sickly smell of diesel, smothering the window-box gardens of pansy and mignonette.

"Hirsh!"

But his brother was already at his back. Tanks rolled by beneath them, flanked on both sides by infantry in crisp khaki summer jackets and armbands of brightest red. There were tanks on Strashun Avenue, before eight o'clock on a morning in high summer.

Hirsh pressed a hand to Mikah's shoulder, and he felt it, so it had to somehow be real.

[July 1941]

ALL THE BURNING STARS

"Drunk on the pen trembling in my hand, I record everything . . . "

—H. Kruk

"There's a call for books."

"A what?"

"The Judenrat wants books."

Raissa wailed. "What else can they take from us?"

"No, no, listen. They want to start a library." Fayge kept a distance from the two of them, even after Violeta had unwound her arms from Raissa's shoulders, but her voice was eager. She set a half-loaf of bread and a can of milk on the desk as she spoke, as an offer of strange truce, or an excuse for coming so far down the hill, and out of her own way; Raissa was unsure. But it was white bread.

"I know you have books—"

Raissa left off staring at the sharp edge of crust where the loaf had been divided, and looked at Beniek's wife. Since the Ghetto had been sealed, it seemed, she had not slept; she went about with a half-dreaming cast to her features. Half the days that went by, there was no accounting for her from daybreak to rehearsal's start. Wherever she went, it was not to the bottom of Zydowska Street—*darling, there was a time you too feared the proletariat,* Violeta said, tongue in her cheek—and not to bring news, and bread.

"More books than anyone I know, and I thought you might give something." Fayge smiled, a bit. "I've met the librarian, or one of them. His name's Herr Kruk, and he seems—"

"Kruk is here? In Vilna?" Violeta stood, though it trapped Fayge between the desk and the door, and Violeta was scrupulous on that score.

"Yes. He seems to love words for words' sake," Fayge finished.

"They gave Kruk the library." Her expression hovered between pleasure and disappointment. "A borderless Jewish cultural nation," Violeta murmured, quoting from somewhere, "and it ends in two miles of razor wire, begging for books."

"Pardon?"

"I'm sure we can find something." Sliding sideways, Violeta crouched to draw a tin footlocker from beneath their studio couch. "Take these to him. Here. Please."

"All of them?"

"And . . . " Violeta hesitated, looked from Raissa to the food on the table and back again, breathed hard and bit her lip. She set the can of milk on top of the footlocker. "Give this to Lutski. Khaykl Lutski, the archivist. He'll be there, unless they pried the books from his stiffening hands." She grinned.

"There's no Herr Lutski," faltered Fayge.

"Oh."

*

He was thirty-seven years old, and his hair was silvery white. His eyes, the color of good chocolate, were clear and quick.

He had no jacket or vest or coat, only three or four shirts buttoned one over the other, but the shirts were clean. Instead of an armband he wore a yellow felt star at the level of his heart, inscribed with mock Hebrew. He was taller than Fayge but not so tall as Hirsh; he had a sharp economy of movement that was cautious, but without fear. He took the basket of books before greeting them: a kiss for Raissa's grimed right hand, the left cheek and then the right for Fayge.

"You'll need this," Fayge said, untied her armband and pressed it into his hand. "Sir, the yellow star's no good here."

"They say you were a professor," Raissa cut in. "At a real university . . . "

"Raissa, for God's sake!"

"I just wanted to know," she stepped back onto Fayge's foot, "whether we're to call you Doctor, Professor—"

"Call me Kruk," he suggested. "It's my name." He smiled, a very tired gesture that never reached his eyes. "If I was doctor, professor, it was all very long ago." Kruk turned to unpack their basket; he flipped slow and reverently through Raissa's collected Shakespeare, and smoothed the binding of Fayge's Schiller. There were already rough shelves set up, as high as Raissa could easily reach, and she left Fayge standing in the doorway and went to them. Empty, for the most part, and with sap still oozing from the boards, but there were twenty or thirty books, well cared for, well-bound in crimson and green and indigo leather. Half of them were printed, along the spine, in alphabets she didn't understand. Raissa chose the slimmest and smallest volume, with no letters at all on the spine; she wiped her hands on her shirt-tails and pulled it from the shelf.

The joy of a new book pushed away hunger, pain, and cold; she opened the book to the middle and buried her nose and breathed in the paper. Smoke from a wood fire, lilac or rose water, and good ink . . .

Something slipped from the pages, and fell with a crisp little sound to the floor.

It was a photograph. Raissa picked it up by the edges, so as not to smear the tints; but the colors seemed to be fast in the paper itself. A woman, smiling, calm, worlds away, in a garden in autumn; the trees showed gold as well as deep green. Her dress was white and her pelisse was warm dark red, and a book was open under her left hand. She had only begun to smile.

Along the white edge at the bottom someone had written, in an angular Roman hand, "S. Paris, 13.10.34."

Raissa tucked the photograph back in its place, and came out from amongst the shelves. Kruk's back was to her, his broad white shoulders and whiter hair stark in the gathering gloom.

"Sir, please," she whispered, shy of interrupting him.

"You read Sappho?" He took the little volume from her hands.

"I know of her, sir, I can't read this, I think it's Greek," stammered Raissa. "Only I didn't think this was meant to be in it." She nudged the photo out, onto the table where Kruk had begun stacking volumes.

His palm covered it, and his fingers curled round, and the table and the books and the lamp tilted, heaved up, to smash and scatter with a terrible noise. Fayge cried aloud when the room lost its light, and froze where she was; Raissa found the lamp by burning her fingers on it, and blew on the wick until something rose that might be called a flame.

Kruk sat amidst the ruin, on top of books, with books digging into his back and pyramided under his knees. Because the lamplight caught them, Raissa knew his eyes held tears; but he wept without a harsh breath or a sound.

*

"This one's got pages missing," said Raissa. "And this one, here, it's burnt or something. He can't mean to have these in a library."

Fayge took the two volumes and propped them on a half-empty shelf. They were textbooks, with plain grosgrain covers, one in English, one in Polish. They had been well-kept once, though now the bookplates had been ripped from them and their corners split and curled. The fly page of the English book was crumpled and filthy, as though the book had lain sprawled-open; the Polish text was scarred burnt-brown, and the color plates were sagging away from binding too badly split to take their weight.

Fayge smoothed back the flyleaf of the Polish text, frowning.

It was marked, neatly, in the upper right corner, *K. S.*

"No," Fayge said, "I don't think these are meant for the library."

"Why would he keep them? Wouldn't get a zloty for the both."

For a second, Fayge stared. "He keeps them because of his wife."

"Oh." Raissa looked subdued. She picked up an illustration plate that had fallen from one of the books, and tucked it away. "I wonder why the professor's wife had an anatomy book. And English, of all things! Do you suppose she liked figure drawing?"

Fayge gathered the books and set them away and stepped whispering-close to Raissa. "Idiot, don't you know what happened to his wife?"

"No!" Raissa blinked.

She shook her head. A glance down the shelves revealed Kruk at his desk, with the lamps lit, marking in the ledger of borrowers, borrowed, owed. Fayge shifted so that her back was between him and any sound, and went on.

"His wife taught at the medical school in Warsaw, until the Germans came. They closed the University, and threw the teachers out in the road. The students all had to go in labor brigades." Fayge's pale eyes were distant, as if she saw stone towers and brick pathways instead of green-pine shelves. "Some of the teachers decided not to stop teaching. They made a University, even a medical school, all in secret. Underground?" Fayge paused, to question the Yiddish.

"But it's death," Raissa interrupted. "You can't."

"They did. I don't know. I wasn't there. Herr Kruk says—all kinds of classes, in any place you could think of. Political science in the greengrocer's, chemistry in a church. He didn't say where she was teaching," Fayge steadied herself, "when they caught her."

"Oh, God. They shot her."

"No." Fayge ran a hand over the cool, still, ragged pages of the books. "They shot the students. They threw her out of a window."

After some time, Raissa cleared her throat. "Fayge? What was her name?"

"I don't know. He's never told me."

[September 1941]

It was one of those cool, interminable afternoons when no rain fell, when none of the Jewish Police brought edicts on stiff paper; the library was closed, with all the ideas, all the new, all the fresh plays and songs locked inside it. No one had ideas. No one even made any good mistakes. There was nothing to do but swallow hunger and keep on working, marking time until Beniek lit the lamps against the theatre's dark. Hirsh had gone below to the orchestra pit, and paced out his frustration between the scattered chairs and music stands; Raissa and Violeta had taken a candle and left the stage for the privacy of

113

the wings, to salvage the last act of the new revue with red ink and cleverness neither one felt.

"Raissa, leave us, please."

Startled, Raissa had her mouth half open for the retort when she saw Beniek. She got up, then, accepting his hands to pull herself onto her feet, and Violeta set down the red-ink bottle and the lines she was editing and managed to look unsurprised. Beniek did not offer her a hand up.

Beniek never spoke to her, if he could help it; nor she to him. They stood, neither slouching, and regarded each other in superb and polite discomfort. They moved uneasily, rounding each other's space as if they were fencing, not talking.

"You were a teacher before the war. My sister's teacher."

"Yes."

"The Judenrat wishes you to teach again." Beniek studied her reaction, such as it was, the quick lowering of her brow, the set of her mouth.

"I've never taught children," Violeta said. "I wouldn't know where to start."

"Not children. We—the Judenrat would like to offer a Russian class, for those who wish to learn. I've told them you speak Russian. I know you're . . . good at languages."

"Passably," said Violeta, beginning to smile.

"To hell with passably, I've heard you."

"Had you? I hadn't noticed."

"I've told them you're qualified," he reiterated, because he did not know how to reply when she smiled like that, just one corner of her mouth turned up in utter amusement. "It won't be—I should tell you—without some risk."

"I'm not afraid." She came one step closer to him. She was tall; she could meet his eyes. "But the risk won't touch Raissa, understand that."

"I think we are agreed on that count."

"Oh, good, I was beginning to fear we had nothing to talk about." Violeta kept her pronouns as formal as his, but it seemed behind all the stiffness she was seconds away from a laugh. "I'll need paper, pencils, someplace with good light, and let's say five or six sugar coupons, just for fun. She likes chocolate."

"She?"

"Your sister."

"The Judenrat has classroom space arranged."

"I love her, you know, more than my own life."

"Pencils, paper, I can make no guarantees."

"You always seemed to doubt that," she continued.

"This is more under the table than above it," Beniek admitted, clearing his throat.

"Do you dislike me so much because she's your favorite, or because I make a bad husband?"

"I'll tell the Judenrat you agree, then. Starting Thursday."

[October 1941]

It was the first of May. The day might have come from a picture, from before: perfect sunlight, smooth bowl of sky. On Strashun Avenue women were selling red carnations, red anemones, and Raissa had knotted a posy of red into her wild dark hair. She walked with Herr Kruk's hand at her elbow, guiding her steps down the steepest part of the hill. Hirsh was behind, and when she started to sing the Internationale, he had to sing, too, to drown her out.

The street was packed, flooded with schoolchildren though it was not past noon. The crowd, down the sidewalks and in the gutters and between the rickshaw wheels, began to press the three of them, and though people were laughing and some picked up the singing, there was something else now in the air.

Raissa dropped back to speak to him, and the laughing line of her mouth was tempered by anxiety. "Hirsh? Something's going to happen, Hirshke; I don't like it."

Kruk turned, too; the spring breeze flicked his white hair. He stood at a right angle to Hirsh, to keep Raissa from being swept away down the hill, and looked back the way they had come. There was no way up the hill again.

"It'll be all right," he said. "It's May Day."

It defied logic, to Hirsh, but Kruk lifted Raissa onto his shoulder and she laughed again, for surprise, for joy. It was enough to make Hirsh follow them down to the bottom of the street.

The kitchens were closed. The doors were shut. In front of them, a ragged, random three-piece band had come together: an accordion player, a man with a child's drum, and a youth with a violin. They played workers' songs, Bund songs, brave and happy tunes, and if the accompaniment sounded thin, the voices all around them made up for it. The kitchens were closed. There was no prospect of food, and people were singing. Hirsh stood with one hand on Raissa's knee, steadying her, and did not sing; his eyes were on the young man and the violin.

He knew that fiddle, knew the red-gold of its lacquer, knew best of all the faded blue ribbon tied below the pegs. The ribbon had been Raissa's, years ago, and the instrument had been his brother's.

"Mikah," he said, "Mikah."

The youth's fingers slid skilled and lively on the strings, and Mikah was dead. For a moment the cry of *grave robber, thief* was bitter in Hirsh's mouth.

But Mikah had loved his instrument too well to take it into danger with him, Hirsh thought, and his anger broke. He had left it somewhere safe, in the care of friends, and his friends did him the honor and the fiddle sang again . . . That young man, with his wrist-bones sharp as stones, with the daze of hunger in his eyes but the flush of playing to brighten his face, had known Mikah. Hirsh would speak to him, when the music was over, when the crowd thinned.

Too soon, the band stopped playing. The crush of thin bodies around the kitchens' doors had swelled to overwhelming; those who had come expecting lunch, and those who had come to keep the holiday, were pressed so fast together in the courtyard of 2 Strashun that even with the wind off the river, it was growing hard to breathe.

The man with the violin set it back in its case—Mikah's case, with the gouge down it from being thrown in the river—and leaned the case in the shelter of the doorway. He stood, and wiped sweat from his hands, and spoke. "Workers! Sisters! Brothers!"

Raissa, up on Kruk's shoulder, cheered and clapped, and she was not alone.

"Raissa." Hirsh tugged on her trouser leg. "Raissa, who is that boy?"

"That's Wittenberg, Isaac Wittenberg," she replied, a little breathless. "He's not a boy, he's a partisan, he's commander of the FPO!"

The papers spoke of him, the enemy spoke of him, Mikah had spoken to Hirsh of him. Hirsh had expected a colossus, a real partisan, not a fiddler boy with roses in his cheeks.

"I tell you there will be no peace, not this year, and that we can no longer stand here while they take our lives." Wittenberg had made his voice swell to encompass the whole crowd, or else the crowd had stilled. "Today is the worker's holiday. Look around you and see how few workers are left! This place—the heart of our people in all of Europe! This city is echoing, and empty, and in the night where there was music once, your murdered children are crying!"

117

"I've heard this speech before," whispered the professor, "but that boy's damned good."

Raissa put a hand down to grip Hirsh's shoulder, because he could not tear his eyes from Wittenberg or the violin.

"Where are the Jews, sisters, brothers? No one will ask it, now, but the Jews! Where are thirty thousand of us who danced in this street last year? Jews, I beg you, fight for what you love! Fight for your lives!"

The people were held hushed, but there was a sound, behind them, thin and strange muffled by all the bodies, but coming closer.

"Jews!" Isaac Wittenberg shouted. "Defend yourselves with arms!"

Horses, the sound was of horses.

"Murer!" Someone screamed, raw, high with terror, and there was the crack of a pistol shot. In the tumble and tumult, Hirsh lost sight of Wittenberg; there were five men on horseback, Murer and Kittel at the fore riding down like death. Death was their coats and their hands and their pistols, their faces and their beasts, and they rode women and the smallest children beneath them as they came on. People fell and were paving-stones, and three mounted men of the Jewish Police were firing straight into the crowd.

Kruk threw Raissa into the crowd, out of harm's way; the second's delay put him in the path of Murer's truncheon, the glass-studded one, and he fell with red blooming through his white hair. In half a second he would end, Hirsh knew, under the hooves of Murer's horse —

"Professor!" Hirsh did the only sensible thing, or maybe the worst thing, but he was doing it before any thought. He grabbed the creature's bridle nearest the bit and pulled. The horse screamed, the rider unbalanced, and Hirsh got the horse's jaw hard against his own and went flying. But no one had been crushed.

Hans Murer was down on the cobblestones, his black cloak flung out, his black and silver hat a arm's span away. He did not move.

"Gottenyu," someone muttered, around the blood in Hirsh's mouth; he had spoken, he realized, and Raissa was dragging on his arm. "Wait," he pleaded with her. "Wittenberg. . ."

"Never mind it," she commanded, and now Kruk was beside him as well. His hair was white, but he was not old; he ran faster than Hirsh would have ever believed. "Run!"

*

"Wittenberg got away," said Raissa, and handed him a wet cloth for his head. "They shot nine people, Hirsh, and there will be more tonight."

"Murer?"

"Still alive."

"Fuck," said Hirsh. Raissa jumped back. "What does the *Geto-Yedies* say?"

"That the waste of life is senseless and shameful."

"What does the FPO say?"

Raissa grinned. "The leaflet's just come up, all over the Ghetto."

"And?"

"Sell your goddamned lives dear."

Hirsh nodded, thoughtfully.

[May 1942]

"You haven't touched your soup."

"It's turnip. I hate turnip," Hirsh said, but he took some broth, to please her. The spoon bumped the corner of his mouth as if he could not be bothered to guide it.

"Mazek, what's on your mind?"

Hirsh shook his head. "Maybe I can't eat with you scratching away like that."

Raissa set down her pen, and capped the ink, an instant before he dipped his spoon for it. "No more work, then," she agreed, "but it's something. Tell us."

Fayge was marking sheet music, with a stub of something greasy and faint, and eating all the while; she started, when Raissa said *us*, but paid attention.

"I don't know." Hirsh shifted on the bench, drawing one knee to his chest, and propped his arm on his threadbare trousers and fussed at the ties of his armband. "I don't know. All of this. I can't get my head around it any more."

"None of us can get our heads around it," said Raissa quietly. "We'd die, or go mad."

"We just sit here," muttered Hirsh. "We eat this swill, once a day, it's not enough to keep us alive—look at us, Rais'le, I don't think you're supposed to die slow enough for people to see it!"

She braced a hand on his back, because shouting took so much energy now, and he'd started shaking.

"We ought to do something, fight, kill them, I don't know, we ought to do something."

"A foreigner, a cripple and a . . . whatever you are, a poet?" Amused, or bemused, Fayge gestured with her spoon.

"Whatever I am," Hirsh echoed. He was so pale, in these half-ration days, that no color could cross his cheeks, but his hand went to his armband, crushed and tore it off.

"Hirsh, put the damn thing back on!" Fayge nearly bolted up from the table. The soup kitchen's Jewish Police carried only truncheons, but the crowd at lunchtime earned two Arrow Cross, one for each end of the hall, and their rifles were in their hands, not on their backs.

"Why should I?"

"Because you carry your proof in your trousers even so, and you really don't want them looking there!"

Raissa took up the armband, slid it around his bicep and tied it, speaking very softly. "If it's Wittenberg you've got stuck in your head, go and see him."

"You can't just go and see the FPO!"

"You could." Raissa ducked her head, to the left, right, behind, but their table was empty and the scrape of five hundred spoons careened off the walls. "Violeta told me, once, Itsik Wittenberg loved your brother; he sent him all the places he couldn't go, himself, because they were such friends. Ask Fayge. She feeds them. Ask Fayge."

"I would have known something like that!"

"No," Fayge replied, perhaps a little sadly. "You wouldn't. But they were friends. If you wanted to find him, your name would get you through."

Hirsh turned on Raissa, not Fayge. "You're saying my brother was—that he was from the other riverbank, like you!"

"I'm not saying that!" Raissa corrected, astonished, "I'm saying Wittenberg trusted him, and he'll trust you." She looked up from her notebook, straight at him. "If he was like me, would that be the worst thing?"

"Yes!"

Her inked hand strayed up to her mouth, as if he had hit her there. She did not call after him when he left. Instead she gathered her things, sweeping pen into notebook without wiping the nib, so a black smear trailed her corner of the table.

"Where are you off to?" Fayge finished licking the back and hollow of her spoon, and set it in the bowl.

"The library."

"It can wait until you eat!"

"I'm not hungry," growled Raissa. "I want to see the professor."

"You'll never cross the bridge at this hour; everyone's coming to eat, you'll get knocked down." Fayge reached across the table for Hirsh's half-plate of soup, and divided it between theirs. "Finish. It's potato, not turnip. If you finish, I'll walk you to the library myself."

Lured by a piece of boiled potato at least the size of a snail, Raissa sank back to the bench. She cut the potato carefully in two with the edge of her spoon, considered, and ate. "You talk to me like your two-year-old."

Fayge shrugged. "That's not true. I say *sie* when I think of it."

"Not what I meant." Raissa glowered down at a cabbage fragment. "Idiot, moron, *gonif.*"

"He loved his brother. He loves you."

"Hirsh?" Raissa snorted. "Not in a thousand years."

[June 1942]

"Hirshke! Mazek!" Raissa shouted over the whine of the machines. He did not immediately see her, paused like a black-and-white island between head-high banks of whirring bobbins; when he did he took off his apron, and held out his stained hands.

"Raissa, what are you doing here? What's going on?" Close by her ear, careworn concern. He looked for the dipper and bucket, to offer her water.

"I'm visiting the foreman," she replied, as if coming a mile and a half in such heat was a pleasure stroll. "Herr Kruk sent me, with the atlas you wanted. Look, all wrapped, no grubby finger prints."

"You're not grubby. You're short." He took the parcel, and kissed both her cheeks.

"Not the mouth!" she cried warning. "You'll get my bloody cough."

Caught, or burned, or bee-stung, he backed away. "Come downstairs," said Hirsh, "it's cooler." She had torn the sleeves off this shirt, at the start of summer; her remaining muscles stood out ropy against the bones, and he hesitated now to take her bare arm, or offer his.

Raissa put her hand in his, instead, to be led among the machines. They said nothing as they crossed the shop floor, because it was useless in all the noise. When she leaned on him to get down the dim flight of stairs, she did so without asking or needing to ask.

"How is your back?" Hirsh waited until his ears had stopped ringing, and his eyes had adjusted for lack of light.

"The way it always is," she replied. "Shot to hell. Do you mind, can I sit? Floor's fine."

He dragged out a few sacks of lint, instead, arranging them like armchairs and ottomans. "My parlor."

"The perks of management," Raissa grinned. "You're kidding, they save lint?"

"God knows what they do with it, except pile it in the cellar." Hirsh shrugged. "You didn't have to walk so far, just to bring me a book."

"Oh, I was bored."

"I would have come to you."

"I know." She sprawled on her sacks, with her head near his ribs. "Hirsh, I felt like walking. If it makes you feel better, put me in a rickshaw when I leave; but I always feel sorry for the poor man doing the pulling."

"Faster, coolie, please," Hirsh quoted, half in song.

"I'd never tell them to go faster. My God."

"I know, but you're well-bred." He dug in his pockets for some bread, found none, and stretched at his length looking mournful. "I'm sorry, I've nothing to offer you."

"Nothing I'd take from you," she said, unthinking. When she did think, for a moment, she put her hand out and met with his collar, and he was trembling.

"Hirsh, no, I didn't mean that."

"It was the truth." His voice came a little stiffly, as if it caught on something.

"You're my friend, Hirshke. Always, my friend. And—in another life, maybe, more than that. If I could be like that, Mazek, it would be with you. I've tried to be like that, and I can't."

"I spoke to your father," Hirsh said, flat.

"You spoke to—you braved Father? Why? When?"

"The usual reason." He coughed. "You were in Berlin."

"Whatever he said to you, Hirsh, I'm sorry. He must have—"

"He didn't turn me down, actually."

"Then why didn't you —" Raissa's face had twisted, all brows and mouth.

"Because I am your friend." He looked apologetic, for interrupting her. "Anyway it was years ago. It doesn't matter."

Raissa stared at him for more than three minutes. He sat silent, folded, his countenance like a bruise. Her voice had a thick rusting sound when she spoke again. "What's the atlas for? It was heavy."

"Herr Kruk can kill me, if he catches me, but I'm going to tear some pages out of it. I need a map."

"A map where?" Raissa sat up, ignoring the pullings and creakings and pain, and laid a steadying hand on his arm. "Hirsh, there's nowhere to go but here."

He shook his head. "Plenty of places. You just have to get there."

"They'll shoot you. Or worse! I don't want to think about

the worse." She covered her face with her hands. They were after all grubby, and suddenly cool with sweat.

"You don't have to think about it, because I won't get caught." Hirsh took her hands down, pressed her damp fingers on his knees. "Listen, they're looking east, always east. The Russians see to that. All I have to do is get out of here and go somewhere else. North," he suggested.

"Oh, God."

"You could come with me . . . "

"I can't ride, I can't swim, I can't run," she deterred him. "I'll be all right, here. You said it yourself: the Russians are barely over the border."

"I don't want to leave," he said suddenly, the brightness faltering from him. "Rai, I can't. I had all these thoughts of—of finding the Partisans, fighting the Germans, just being out there, being free—and I can't!"

"You can," she snapped. "You'd better. If you know a way out of here, you take it! And you do have a way, or you wouldn't risk a library book."

"But—"

"I think you're mad as hatters, all right, and I think it's dangerous, but it never crossed my mind," she lied, "that you couldn't do it."

"But I never thought of it," Hirsh persisted. "Me getting away from here, and you . . . not."

"I'll be all right," she went on lying, boldly. "I'll be here when you get back."

"How can you say something like that?"

"What, do you want me not to?" Raissa leaned in and kissed, very precisely,the corner of his mouth. He had never been closer to her in his life, and he couldn't move. Not until she pulled away.

"Raissa. . ."

"Go, then," she looked straight into his eyes, unflinching, as if that would vanish him from the Ghetto inside a second. "But promise to come back."

[September 1942]

AFTER THE END
OF THE WORLD

" . . . a song written in blood, not lead . . . "
—H. Glik

"Hirshke!"

He had only half lowered himself through the window; the cry made him scrabble and stiffen and drop the rest of the distance into a bone-rattled heap. Raissa was across the green room, with her arms around him, so quickly her chair smacked back-first onto the floor.

"What did you do to your hair?" Raissa's glad cry trailed off into dismay.

"Peroxide," he said, instead of hello.

"Or something." Fayge winced. "My God, your feet."

"Never mind his feet! Look at his hair!"

Hirsh straightened, one hand covering the white-bleached wreckage. An old man he looked, or a spirit long leached, but not a Pole. Rags crossed the insteps of his boots, and the straps of his rucksack had cut into his army coat. He wore a small-caliber rifle, badly.

"What are you doing here?"

"Where have you been?"

" . . . Water?"

Fayge came to him, with the bucket and dipper; he took the bucket, and drank.

"You're out of your mind," she said, to the upturned bucket. "Coming here in daylight! Armed! Where did you walk from? Where did you cross? How in hell do you intend to get back to the frontier?"

"Listen," he said at last, gasping around the last mouthful of liquid. "Listen to me. They're taking everyone. Whatever money you have, it's not enough." Hirsh stuck a hand into his coat, and drew out a greasy and much-folded sheet of paper. It was typewritten, and no one had used the margins. Clear black at the top of the page was the cruel-beaked eagle of the General Government.

Raissa touched it first. She put on her eyeglasses one-handed, using her teeth on the earpieces, as if something sealed her right hand to the paper. "I don't understand," she said. "I don't know what it means. To liquidate?"

Fayge, unbalanced, gripped Raissa's shoulder. "It means the Ghetto is over," she said. "It means our death." She was a little paler, her eyes a little wider, than Raissa had ever seen; when she spoke again, all Fayge's attention was for Hirsh. She had drawn the wallet from her bodice without thought, and her small nimble fingers were sliding over the bills. Fifteen thousand marks, twenty thousand, fifty.

"How old is the order?"

"More than a week already," Hirsh looked apologetic. "I walked from Siauliai, and I lost two days playing hide and seek with some snipers across the river."

"Stay here," ordered Fayge. "Out of sight. I have to—I have to—"

"I've been to the Judenrat. I've spoken to Herr Kruk. They already know. And I've seen the trains—trains enough for thousands—from the southwest."

"Kruk? What about Jakob Gens?"

"No one can find Herr Gens."

"Then he's not alive," said Fayge, "and no help's going to come."

Raissa had been sitting silent, her fingertips in her mouth; now she hauled upright. "You're talking over my head," she said simply. "But I'm still here. Why would Hirsh have walked miles and miles, if there's no hope of help?"

"To get you out," he replied, with no mention of hope at all.

"But the Russians," Raissa persisted. "They can't be far. You can't lie down at night, for the artillery!"

"That's why they're in such a hurry." Fayge gave a vicious little smile. "Read for yourself. If nothing's happened to change that order, the Ghetto will be rags and ashes by tomorrow night."

"And we just walk out? We pay our bribes and leave, right now, just leave?"

"Rais'le," Hirsh hushed her.

"What happens to everybody else?"

Fayge never flinched. "Treblinka happens. You want to stay here and wait?"

"Your daughter—"

" . . . is safe out of their reach." She frowned for a moment, passed a hand through her hair, and was calm. "Hirsh, here's ten—fifteen thousand. Take her to the north gate. Time enough to get out that way, before the light goes."

"What the hell am I? Potatoes in a sack?!" Raissa's cheeks were bright with rage. "We have to warn people! We have to—"

Hirsh took her hand. His eyes, darkened green-gray with tears, held shouts of pain and anger, but his mouth was shut.

After a moment Raissa fell silent, under his silence. Her throat worked and trembled, but the words had fled with his.

Because she could think of nothing else to do, she took the bread ration from her pocket and put it in Hirsh's hand. "You've not eaten."

"No," he said. "Thank you."

*

They carried nothing, and left the great doors of the theatre wide open to the day's heat. The streets were sun-filled and sleepy. Hirsh kept Raissa's hand in his, and behind them came Fayge, wary and wire-tensed with her own hands deep in the pockets of her faded coat.

"We're going to walk through the gate?" Raissa blanched. "Hirshke . . . ?"

"We're going to pay them a lot of money to walk through the gate," he corrected. "And cold cash is worth more than Jews, and we'll be all right."

Halfway up the hill here were voices close behind them, and the words were not Yiddish. The sound floated up towards them, as they kept walking, without daring pause, into the sun. No question but they were seen; no chance, now, of passing unchallenged under the guns at the gate. Raissa felt Fayge's hand at her back.

"Don't turn. Don't run until I say."

Hirsh ducked left, when Fayge pressed him, into the stark shade of the ancient archways that had shaped the ghetto once, three hundred years before. The gate was lost to them, and booted feet and voices still coming behind.

"It's no good," Fayge groaned, lost and tired and young. Ahead of them was only the pale stone and plaster of the old ghetto's outer wall, crumbling, six meters high and without purchase for even the most desperate climb.

"We can't stand here and wait for them!"

"Which way do you want us to go, up?"

Hirsh flattened into a corner, out of the light, frantic, planning or praying with dark slimy water running from the pores of the wall into his hair.

"You've got fifty thousand marks on you," Raissa gasped out, "and he's got a rifle! Hide, for God's sake! You'll get shot!" She shoved at Fayge and turned, back under the archway, within sight of the gate; she stood still for a moment, cursed herself for a madwoman and changed direction, a harmless, small, shambling kind of run, and towards the men in black and silver, not away.

"A Jew-girl running! Like a stumbling duck!"

"Where are you running to? Speak up!"

"I work at the theatre," Raissa wheezed, truthful enough. "I'm late for rehearsal."

"There were more of you, a second ago."

"No. Just me." She cast a glance over her shoulder, shrugging, and indeed the alley was empty. " 'S nothing back that way, anyway, no one lives up here any more . . . "

"Papers!"

Languid, outside herself with fear, she got a hand around the worn leather wallet, willed the fingers to close. Something else fell from her pocket, and the wind caught it up and carried it, fluttering, white, but she managed to hand over her papers.

What had slipped from her was not a handkerchief. It was Hirsh's stolen order, and the eagle on it was still black and startling. One of the soldiers stopped it with his boot.

Raissa screamed, once, when they caught her by the hips and by the hair. Dragged sideways, bloody-mouthed, she found the cobbled road against knees and palms. Sound swallowed everything, a crack, a roar, small clinks of metal on the stones, like falling coins. A wetness was on her, all down her back, strange hot sweat, and she was no longer kneeling. The sky came down onto her chest. She fell.

*

"Raissa. Raissa!"

She moaned, when Hirsh called to her, and one hand opened and grasped at nothing, until Hirsh took it. He hushed her and begged her and would have taken her in his arms but Fayge was quicker, already crouched with Raissa's head on her lap; she lifted the dark tangle of Raissa's hair and saw the face drained white, and the purpling blood that came on each breath.

"I've never seen so . . . " Fayge turned her face aside, teetering between sorrowful and sick. Then like a spark in the sunlight her knife flashed, quick as the will she set to it. Hirsh roared, wordless, and the blade met his forearm instead of Raissa's throat.

"She can't live," Fayge protested, unheeded, aggrieved.

"She doesn't need your help to die!" Hirsh stroked back her hair, cautiously. Her eyes were open, and bright; her bloodied teeth were set hard together. He could see, tracing burnt-black holes in her shirt, where the first bullet had thrown her and twisted her up to embrace the second, a dark shining warmth spreading down her trouser leg and staining his own clothes.

"Hirsh," she said, clearly enough to startle him back on his heels.

"I'm listening. Rais'le."

But there was nothing else, though he bent to her, kissing-close. Foam came crimson to her lips where words might have been; she squeezed his hand, hard. Then Fayge was murmuring something, to Hirsh, to him; and Raissa's eyes were sightless, but the sun and sky were in them.

Fayge cried.

Blood was on her coat, on her hands and Hirsh's. She let him into the apartment, let the key crash on the floor, and stood and cried. There was half a kettle of water, rust-tinged, on the unlit stove; Hirsh poured two inches into the basin on the windowsill and the rest into a glass from which she did not drink. He took her hands, very awkwardly, and while she wept the water in the basin turned pink.

"Here," she said, coming back to herself, and he dropped his handkerchief in the water. Hard enough to press a blood-bruise into her palm, though he had not seen her take it, she held Raissa's ring.

"I didn't think the snatchers should have it," she explained.

"My brother made these." Hirsh was hoarse, though it was high August, and his eyes stung, though the rest of his skin was numb. "Made them look like silver, I don't know how. It's just iron, just a bit of pipe—"

He was talking to give Fayge time; time for what, he didn't know. She stared straight out at nothing, her lashes thick and dark with salt. As she had let Hirsh take her hands, she let him take the ring, and tears dripped off her chin.

Hirsh shifted, foot to foot in his cracked patched boots, and to keep from looking at her face, he looked at the apartment. In the corner to the left, the bedstead, and the bed was made; there was a trundle made from an orange box, but in the summer light from the window, dust dully furred its sheets. To his right, Raissa's studio couch, not made up, coverlet trailing the floor, pillows squashed. The cold stove, the empty cupboard, the desk Fayge gripped at one edge, that was all, and it felt empty. The windows were half open, so he could hear the shelling, and Fayge's sobs. The sulfurous smell of the river in summer, the sharp lemony edge of lavender water; and all beneath it, the ink-and-dust scent of Raissa's papers, her books.

"You don't have much time." Fayge startled him.

She wiped her eyes on the sleeve of her great coat. Then she took the coat off, and laid it over the desk. Her shoulders shook, a breath slammed from her hard enough to stir the forgotten pages of a book, and she went still.

In a summer dress of white flowers on blue, she might have come from free Vilna, might have been dropped here by God's white hand, except her cheeks were red from crying and bruises trailed down her bare arms. Something in her face had changed, to Hirsh's eye, something made him remember that she was the youngest of all of them, the last. He could not see her, with her freckled cheekbones and fair plaited hair, with a pistol in the forest; he did not want to see her as a rag, crumpled, staring sightless, under the arch on Strashun. She was something like Raissa's sister.

"Come with us," he offered. "Please."

She was not young, anymore, as she looked. "No," she said.

"What?"

"Thank you." Fayge smiled. "No. I have to see my daughter. You go, while there's still light, and I'll catch you up."

Because he stood there staring, empty-handed, with the rifle biting his shoulder, she touched his arm.

"Come on. I'll take you by safer roads than you know."

[August 1943]

He remembered crouching over the fire to thaw off his ink. He remembered Vitka offering him a slice of toast, dry and tasting of woodsmoke, but hot. Most of the camp had not yet woken; this was the time for writing. Vitka picked out dim little melody lines of old marches on her balalaika, brittle in the cold. There was no second slice of toast.

Then, over their heads, a shriek, and smoke. The fire blew apart, and the ground beneath their feet. Hirsh was spun, tumbled, struck by coals and pine brands. Grass and dirt and roots and snow pattered down on him, if there was such a thing anymore as down, and he remembered thinking, *this is how my brother died.*

Hirsh remembered soldiers, a train, cold like knives in his chest, a metal cup of filthy water that stuck and burned his frost-blackened lips. Then he rattled with fever, packed in among living men and dead, and for a long time there was no memory at all.

He was not dead now. He opened his eyes—grit, and damp—and someone shouted above him. He was lying on what felt like a raw plank, and it was too narrow for him to turn toward the sound. Hands lifted him, by elbows and shoulders, from the bunk. Then there was liquid in his mouth, dark-tasting and too hot. Tea.

Hirsh groaned, but the dream did not fall away.

"Steady on, boy."

He looked up. White hair, and that familiar, level voice, but a face like a skull, with a mould of gray beard around the cheeks. Since dead men grew no beards, this one was alive.

"Professor?"

"You're in Kluga."

The name meant nothing to him, and his head was pounding. "Where's Kluga?"

"It's a *lager*," said someone, "a camp. You got luck, boy? Then you might survive a whole month."

It made him dizzy to look up at all these men, with their white maddened eyes and black-shadowed faces. But the professor, Herr Kruk, was calling to him.

"Hirsh, Hirsh. Stay awake, lad, you're all right."

They gave him more tea, though he wanted bread. Once

Kruk had spoken, so did his companions: men who looked familiar, who might have been eighteen or eighty, who Hirsh had long thought dead.

"You were in Vilna, at the end?"

"What happened to them?"

"Were there Jews left?"

"And the FPO, did they rise?"

"What happened to them?"

But Hirsh would not answer that question until Kruk asked it, himself, and his asking was like snow in pine trees.

"Hirsh, what happened to them?"

He turned his face aside, and wept.

[March 1944]

It was sleep salvaged from inside a fevered cavern of pain, but Hirsh slept, when they had left him, after a while. He kept his broken hand stiff across his knees, not that the knit of bone would matter tomorrow morning. His coat was still good enough to keep the cold from his back, and as for hunger, sleep was kind.

He opened his eyes in a house that had never been. There was a warm white drift around him of pillows and quilts, and a window beside his head that opened onto the garden, drenching the bed in the purple scent of late lilacs.

She slept with her back to him, her black hair in its fall of half-curls fired to red in the sunlight. Or maybe she had been waking all along: when Hirsh put out a hand, a clean well-kept hand, and drew the quilt down from her bare shoulder, she shouted.

"Cold!" Indignant, she turned to him.

"Raissa," Hirsh gasped.

"*Gonif*, your hands are freezing. All of you is freezing," she amended.

"Rais'le."

"Hirshke, what's wrong?"

Her name broke from him again, on a sob. She sat up, imperfect, pale; he saw two silvered scars across her stomach. Then she took his hands and kissed him, slow and sweet and fearless as if her mouth had known his life-long.

"I never kissed you," he remembered, and it hurt. "And now I'm dreaming."

"I don't care." Her face had never been pretty, unless she was smiling; she smiled now. Shrugged, and slipped an arm around his neck. "Try again if you want."

Everything around him was clean, bright warmth; he felt the feather mattress under him, and his own hands on her skin. The wounds that killed her had scarred over clean, and she was joking with him.

He kissed her again, though it meant waking, breaking the spell.

She stayed.

"I love you," Hirsh said. He felt the blood heat his ears, but kept speaking, because there was so little time, because it was a dream. "I love you. I miss you. I'm scared out of my mind."

"You're not scared to die." She gave it as truth, and it was.

"No. Just the part that comes immediately before."

"Pain doesn't last."

"What does, Rais'le? For God's sake."

"People."

There were pillows at his back, and he was sinking into them. "What?"

"People are real. They last. Even if they die." Raissa brushed the hair from his forehead, not blood-caked but fine and clean. She had drawn up a featherbed, to add to her own warmth across his chest, and she curled in the shelter of his ribs like a well-contented cat.

"Don't," he begged her, "don't let me fall asleep. If I sleep, I'll wake up, you'll be gone . . . "

"I won't."

Rain was kissing his eyelids when he woke, but he was warm, and where she had touched him the pain had ebbed. There were birds, not too far off, singing; dawn was, maybe, a half hour distant, and even torturers were prompt in this place. Hirsh hunched in his concrete box and counted his breaths, to mark the rest of his time.

*

"Bare your heads!"

His head was already bare, and his hands were bound behind him; he had nothing to do but listen to the susurrus of three hundred prison caps whipped off in the sunny morning. The day was already growing fine and hot, though every night was cold here, and there was a scent of rye and forests on the breeze. Hirsh could see the gallows.

They were crude, the gallows of Kluga, no drop, no hood for the hangman to hide his shame. Maybe he was not ashamed, since he would get a double ration of soup. Just uneven stairs, of bowing dried-out wood, up to a platform high enough for every prisoner to see. Just a ladder, and a noose. The camp drummer, who was no more than fifteen years old, stumbled in his rhythm when Hirsh stumbled on the stairs.

There was no more escape. His feet were already scraping the first rungs of the ladder, and he balked. Strong men, never starved, hauled Hirsh up the rest of the way.

The rope was thicker than he had thought.

"The Jew Glik . . . day of August, nineteen-forty-four . . . trying to escape."

He thought of the men he had killed. He thought of Raissa. Of paper, ink, songs, words. He thought of words.

He could still speak, even now.
Hirsh breathed deep.
He jumped.

[August 1944]

MARTYROLOGY

We spoke in letters of fire, wrote in flame
dashed black and white as the interstices
of a scroll, crowned and fringed, the void
where all unspoken things gather, all lost
words remain: in smeared ink and dull
lead, on paper faded brown, acid, time's
kindling; the language of cold fingers
and bruised faces, iron rails and the stage
whose plays had only one ending. Ash
blows where words burned: a diaspora
of ghosts. Unwritten lyrics, music half
transcribed; a twist of rusted wire, papers
flaked like bone in the earth. Cobblestones
have forgotten our footsteps, the weight
of our bodies—mouths open to the earth,
eyes open to the sky. A blunted bullet;
a splintered lens. Chips in a brick wall.
The years grow over like grass. We kept
songs like prayers on the tongue, like
curses, the jargon of angels hymned
bitterly while we held each other fast:

hold us now. From lead and gold, we wrote
each other: from fire, sing us now again.

—Sonya Taaffe

REFERENCED WORKS

Arad, Yitzhak. *Ghetto In Flames.* New York: YIVO, 1957 ed.

Gellerman, Raissa. [diary and papers] Privately held, USHMM. 1943 n.p.

Glik, Hirsh, et al. *Lider Un Poems.* [Y] New York: YIVO, 1950 facsimile ed.

Kaczerginski, Schmerke. *Lider fun di getos un lagern.* [Y] H. Lievick, ed. New York: Tsiko-ferlag, 1946.

Kruk, Herman. *The Last Days of the Jerusalem of Lithuania.* Benjamin Harshav, ed. New Haven: Yale University Press, 2002. Trans. Barbara Harshav.

Kalmanowicz, Selig. *A togbuch in Vilne-Geto.* [Y] YIVO-bleter 35: 18-92, 1951.

Rudashevski, Itshok. *The Diary of the Vilna Ghetto.* Israel: Beit Lohamei haGetaot, 1973. Trans. Percy Matenko.

Sutzkeyver, Abraham. *In vilner geto 1941-1944.* [Y] Paris: Farband fun di vilner in Frankraykh, 1946.

Taaffe, Sonya. "Years Like Yahrzeit Candles." *Electric Velocipede* 8, edited by John Klima, March 2005.

_____., "Martyrology,"first appearance here.

Printed in the United States
43374LVS00007B/3

9 780809 550814